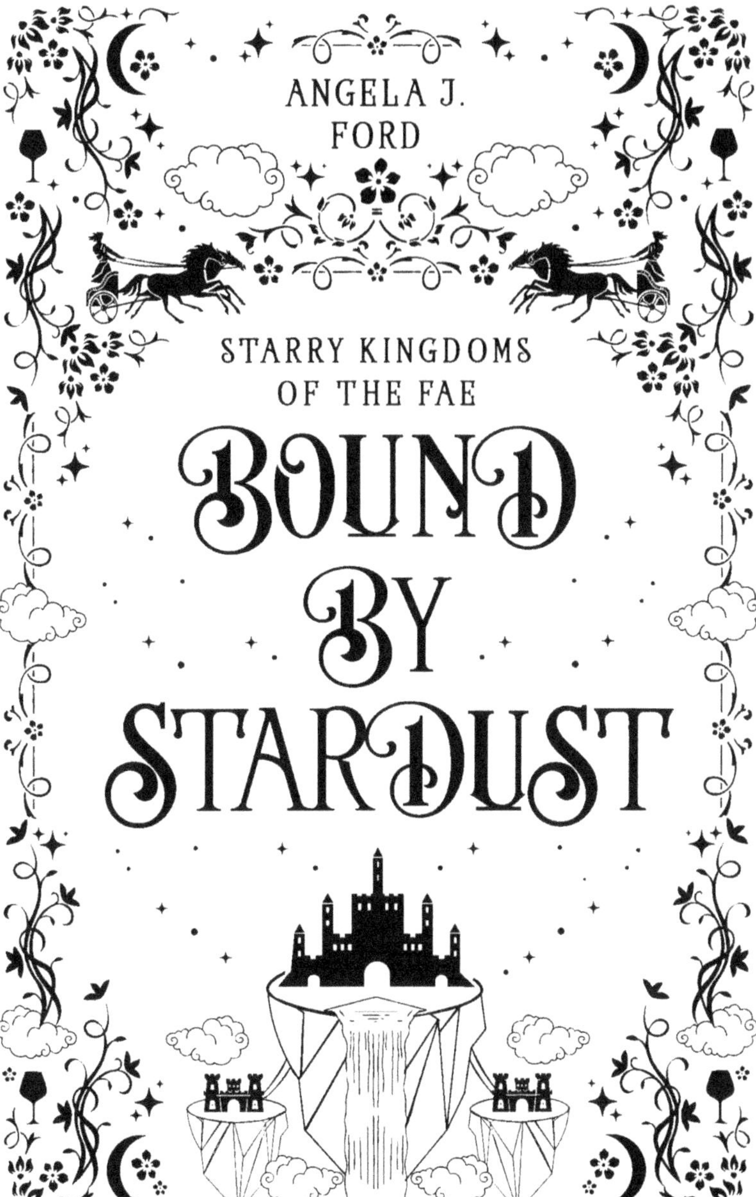
ANGELA J.
FORD
STARRY KINGDOMS
OF THE FAE
BOUND
BY
STARDUST

STARRY KINGDOMS OF THE FAE

# BOUND BY STARDUST

Editing & Proofreading: The Fiction Fix

Cover: Cover Dungeon Rabbit

Case Artwork: Marina Ceban



Visit angelajford.com for more.

# I

# ASIRA

Every year on All Hallow's Eve, stardust fell from the three floating islands, but no one collected the silver and golden motes except for me. Those in the starry kingdom above did not tolerate trespassers, but I'd been gathering stardust for ten years now without incident. I figured others stayed away because of all the bones.

Directly beneath the shadow of the largest island, surrounded by encroaching trees, lay a path of darkness. The slim trees bent over like the fingers of a withered hand, reaching but not quite long enough to scrape against the ground. The sight of that sacred land, covered in coal-black dirt and white bone, was enough to create vivid nightmares.

Ten years did not dispel the creepiness of the area, and I shivered at the gate, reminded of my first night when I was eighteen. I hadn't been alone then, like now.

Gathering my courage and determination, I swung open the gate and marched inside.

Bones crackled under my booted feet, and I flinched, unease creeping up my spine like cold, dead fingers.

I placed five buckets in a circle and stepped back, lifting my face to the sky.

One. Two. Three.

The floating islands appeared like dark blobs in the frosted moonlight, shielding the night's light from beaming down onto the earth. I hated this place and, not for the first time, I wondered why the Masters in the kingdom above ate so much meat. Did they *have* to dump the bones here? Why not elsewhere? I'd found chicken bones and cow bones, even goat horns. Who ate goats? There were other bones, bigger and longer, but I tried my best not to look at them, as Grandmother had instructed.

*Gather the stardust, but don't look down.*

Stardust had magical properties, useful for healing a range of ailments. Each year, I gathered it and worked it into the tinctures I made for the people of Terrin.

Sure enough, I'd timed my entrance perfectly. Light glittered in the air, extinguishing the darkness, and I drew in a deep breath. The creepiness of the boneyard was worth it for this glory. Stardust rained down around me, glowing brighter like fireflies, except it was all colors: gold, silver, white, even red, a collection of dust filling each bucket.

I'd always been curious about the origins of stardust, but my grandmother told me not to question the magic, to just enjoy it. All the same, I had questions. Spreading my arms, I turned around slowly, grinning like a loon.

Something wrapped itself around my ankle and yanked.

I screamed, and I did the one thing I was never supposed to do.

I looked down.

Another scream tore at my throat, but I slapped my hands over my mouth to keep it inside. My eyes bugged out of my head as I stared at a hand: a human hand with short nails and dirt underneath them, attached to an arm.

I swallowed hard. People whispered tales of bodies coming back to life and the undead springing out of the ground on a night like tonight, an eve where bargains could be made between the living and dead.

I followed the arm, which was attached to a shirt covered in that coal black dirt, and I found a body struggling out of the bracken.

Long, stringy hair followed, and then a moan. "Help me."

My heart pounded so hard, I thought I'd pass out.

I'd woken the undead.

Somehow, on a starlit night, the bones had put themselves together and come alive.

My gaze darted to the gate, which was far away, and my buckets weren't even half full. I needed magical remedies to meet my own needs for the coming year, and stardust made all the difference.

Instead of running, I had to deal with this problem. "Who are you?" I snapped, fear making me angry. "I warn you, I'm armed."

I wasn't, but it was the only warning I could think of.

The fingers uncurled from around my ankle and burrowed into the dirt. As the moonlight shifted, I made out a man crawling from under bones, covered with leaves and mud. He collapsed onto his back with a groan and lay sprawled out at my feet. As the stardust brushed against his skin, I got a good look.

He wasn't dead, just very dirty, and instantly, my mind raced. This wasn't magic – this was foul play. His shirt was ripped open, as though he'd been stabbed, but I didn't see any blood. His clothing hung loosely on him. At first, I thought it was torn, but on closer inspection, it appeared rotted. How long had he been in the boneyard?

He was big, too. Long limbs, thick muscle, and his face!

He had deep-set eyes, sharp cheekbones, a high forehead, and a trim beard covering his pointed chin. Thick, black hair trailed in a tangle to his waist.

I bent to study the side of his head, and sure enough, pointed ears confirmed he was no human. He must be one of the Masters, the beings who lived in the floating kingdom above. They came down to Terrin every year for the tithe, clothed in splendor that mirrored the stars. I'd seen them from afar, wearing masks, and wondered what their faces looked like beneath them. Now, I knew.

I stepped back quickly, almost bumping into my buckets. "What are you doing here?"

"Help me," he murmured again.

One of the Masters was lying wounded at my feet. I could, *should*, help him, perhaps gain honor or some kind of blessing from the Masters for helping one of their kind. Why, then, did fear grip me?

Spinning on my heel, I dashed to the gate where I'd left the wheelbarrow. My stardust buckets were surprisingly heavy once full, and I needed to get them through the forest and back home. The man and the buckets would never fit, but at least I could take him home and return for the stardust. Healing him would be quick work; then, I'd send him on his way and request a favor, maybe some sort of blessing for my work. I had to think of what I wanted.

My humdrum life was fine, but not exciting. I'd long ago given up the idea of a husband and babies – I was too old. Once a woman neared thirty years, she was no longer considered young and fertile in Terrin.

Perhaps I shouldn't have been such a recluse. Grandmother encouraged me to get out more, go to the gatherings and celebrations in Terrin, but instead, I'd wandered into the wood to forage or read. So of course, it was my fault I didn't have friends. Sometimes, when I went to market, I heard the children whispering about the odd wild woman who lived in the forest, which was me now that Grandmother was dead.

My lifestyle used to suit me just fine, but more recently, a restlessness hummed beneath my skin. Talking to the birds that came for breadcrumbs and scolding the raccoons and possums who stole fruit and tiny trinkets was getting dull. I kept waiting for something to happen, to change, but each day arrived the same, with requests for healing potions or other demands on my time. Grandmother enjoyed the work, but I was beginning to begrudge it. The problem was, I didn't know what I wanted. Maybe, when I healed the

Master, he might give me an idea of what to wish for.

Trundling the wheelbarrow to the entrance, I paused. The wheels would get stuck between all the bones, so I needed the Master to gain enough strength to make it to the gate. I eyed his long body with a sigh. He was probably too heavy to push through the forest along the rutted path. I was strong, but not *that* strong.

He was sitting up when I returned, eyes closed, face lifted to the stardust falling upon him like a healing rain. He'd taken off his shirt, or the rags had fallen off him. His pants were in terrible shape too, but I'd seen plenty of naked bodies, and the idea of his nakedness did not intimidate me.

"I have a wheelbarrow," I announced. "If you can make it to the gate, I'll take you back to my cottage and heal your wounds."

Golden eyes bored into me. "Thank you," he croaked.

I should have brought water, but I'd forgotten to bring a water skin on my night of labor.

He groaned again, holding his side as he rose to his knees and reached for me.

I gave myself a little shake to keep my courage and prepared for the stink of him. Grandmother never talked much about it, but sick people had a distinct odor. Wounds smelled terrible, especially festering, rotting ones, like the ones I expected him to have.

He slung an arm around my shoulder and leaned rather heavily on me. Nothing but the scent of earth filled my nose. That, and something distinctly masculine. *Strange.*

"Do you recall what happened to you?" I asked as we stumbled across bones to the wheelbarrow.

"Aye," he croaked. "Trouble."

Vague. "Do you have a name?"

"Drazhan. You?"

"I'm called Asira. You're lucky; I'm the Stardust Collector for Terrin, and a healer. You'll be back on your feet in a day or so."

"Asira. My savior."

I grunted in response and helped him into the wheelbarrow. He spread across it with a sigh, arms and legs hanging out. I scowled at how difficult my return journey would be, then glanced back. I'd have to return for the stardust later, but I still snatched one bucket and put it in his lap. "Stardust will help you heal."

Then, summoning all my inner strength, I started the slow journey back home.

My cottage sat in a clearing in the wood, only an hour's walk from the marketplace, but I preferred the appearance of being on the outskirts. I'd left a light in the window for my return, and I parked the wheelbarrow beside the door. I'd take it around back to the barn later.

"We're here," I announced.

Drazhan opened his eyes and groaned as I swung open the door to the cottage. The faint whisper of leaves fluttered along with the scent of lavender.

Embers glowed in the hearth, and I poked at them as I considered what kind of remedy to make for Drazhan. I'd have to examine him to see what injuries he had, but first, I filled a cup with water and returned to him in the wheelbarrow.

"Here, this will help."

He eyed the cup skeptically. "What is it?"

"Just water, for now," I said, grabbing the half-filled bucket of stardust. While he slept, I'd return for the rest.

With a shaking hand, he gulped down the water and dropped the cup over the side of the wheelbarrow. I scowled as I retrieved it. *Rude.*

"Let's get you inside," I muttered as I helped him to the table.

He lay back, chest rising and falling while I lit candles to examine my patient. Try as I might, I couldn't find any wounds or scars. The skin on his chest, albeit dirty, was clear. Was it internal?

I brought him more water and this time, he propped himself up while he drank, his hands steadier. His golden gaze lingered on me, and even though I wasn't one to be uncomfortable, I recalled that I hadn't brushed my hair this morning or bothered to change after spilling a potion down my dress. I must look a sight, even though the one judging me had been buried alive.

To busy myself, I poured stardust into jars, which wasn't as easy as it sounded. "What happened to you?" I asked Drazhan. "You don't have any wounds, at least not that I can see."

When he spoke, his voice was less rough. "I...I...it's hard to remember. I recall being stabbed and then... it was dark, so dark, with so many bones. I got lost in a sea of nothingness and then you, or perhaps it was the stardust, woke me."

I leveled my gaze at him; it wasn't uncommon for people to forget something terrible that happened to them. Probably better that they did, but he was a Master. He should recall what happened to him. "I didn't see any stab wounds."

He pressed a hand to his chest, then peered down at his filthy body. "You must have healed me."

I frowned. "I did nothing, aside from bringing you home and giving you water." My arms were still burning from pushing him through the forest, and I felt quite grumpy about that.

"All the same, you have my thanks."

I didn't want his thanks, and I didn't like the way my body glowed under his praise. To keep from looking at him, I put the stardust on the shelf and started making him a tincture. "You need to rest. I'll make you a drink, and then I have to go collect the rest of the stardust."

He lay back and folded his hands over his chest. Perfectly dirty hands, with long fingers. I shouldn't be staring at his chest, or the way his muscles rippled, but his eyes were closed, and he didn't notice. In all my days of mending wounds, I'd never seen such a perfectly toned body.

He spoke again, jerking me out of my thoughts.

"I'm quite dirty, and I'm lying on your table. I apologize for that."

"Stop apologizing," I snapped as I put the kettle over the fire.

He was silent while I finished the mixture and brought it over to him. Propping himself up again, he drank it down with a sigh. “You are very kind.”

“I’m not kind. I am just doing my job,” I told him honestly.

“All the same,” he said.

“Sleep. It’s healing, since I don’t know about your injuries. In the morning, see how you feel, and we can go from there.”

“Thank you, Asira.”

I watched as his face relaxed; I knew he’d have good dreams. As for me, I had a long night ahead of me. Leaving the stranger on my table, I picked up the wheelbarrow and headed back to the boneyard.

# 2
## DRAZHAN

The scent of peppermint woke me, or perhaps it was eucalyptus. I opened my eyes to dried roots and herbs hanging from the rafters above me, and my night came rushing back. I was in the cottage of the woman, Asira, who had pulled me out of the boneyard, and I felt alive. Relief sang through my veins, underlaid with weariness, even though I'd slept an entire night. Most of it, anyway.

Disdainful brown eyes met mine as I turned my head. It was Asira herself, dressed in the same gown as last night, with the stain on the front of it. She was tall and willowy, with brown skin and a plait of messy, golden-brown hair, but her figure hid surprising strength. She had pushed me through the forest in a strange contraption last night, something she called a wheelbarrow.

I couldn't look away from her, and I realized what a relief it was to look at someone who wasn't wearing a mask. It was as though she were bare, and I could see her soul shining out of her eyes. They were sharp, shrewd, with a slight weariness behind them. Had she slept at all?

"My savior," I murmured.

Her frown deepened as she crossed the room and laid a hand on my forehead. "How do you feel? You're not warm, which means you have no fever, but I assume all your injuries are internal."

I stretched my fingers and toes. "My greatest crime is lying here, covered in dirt on your table. You must think I have no manners."

"You're sick." She shrugged. "I've healed many at my table."

Her indifference stung more than it should have. I was used to women falling at my feet, begging me to make love to them, and she didn't care. I liked her no-nonsense manner and wondered if I might get a smile out of her. “All the same, I could use a bath, if you could point me in the right direction. I assume your husband won’t mind?”

She flinched and stepped back, eyes guarded. Finally, a reaction.

“I have no husband.” She lifted her chin. “But just because I live here alone doesn’t mean I’m not protected. I take care of myself.”

I fought to keep the sly grin off my face. “I meant no disrespect. It was simply an honest question.”

Asira huffed as though she didn’t believe me, then yanked open the door, letting in a stream of sunlight. “The bath is outside, to the left of the house. It’s rather small, so you might not fit. I’ll fill it while you figure out how to get off the table.”

With those words, she marched out the door, leaving me to groan as I rose. I wanted to laugh at her grumpiness, but as soon as I sat up, pain cut me off. So my body *hadn’t* reknitted from being stabbed.

Taking my movements slowly, I stood to my feet and then paused, breathing hard, as though I were an ancient wizard in need of a staff.

Somehow, I hobbled to the door, and as soon as sunlight struck my face, I leaned against the doorframe, breathing in. The air was thick with the scent of herbs, a far cry from the floating islands that smelled of wine and gold and sin. My mouth firmed in a grim line. I didn't want to think about the Masters and what they'd done once they discovered my true reason for masquerading in their kingdom. I'd been so careful, but it wasn't enough.

Hand against the cottage, which was really a log cabin with vines growing over it and flowers blooming on the rooftop, I made my way to the side of the house, where Asira pumped water into a giant, round bucket. Not a tub at all, and no, I wouldn't fit.

She gave a sharp nod when I appeared and gestured to the tub. "It's not cold, but it's not hot either. You'll have to make do with the lukewarm temperature. I have soap that will make you smell like herbs; it's best for you since you're still healing. I sprinkled stardust in the water that will help as well. Soak for a while, and I'll see what clothes I can find for you."

I smirked at her as I loosened my trousers. "How can I thank you?"

Her gaze snapped to my face as I dropped my trousers and slowly stumbled out of them. A vulnerability flickered across her face, but her next question was unexpected. "You're one of the Masters, aren't you?"

I hadn't imagined having this conversation naked, while I climbed into the bucket of sparkling, herb-scented water. What witchery was this? All the same, I didn't look like the humans in Terrin; she would have drawn her own conclusions just by looking at me. "I am," I admitted, sinking into the water.

The makeshift tub was just big enough to hold me, but I had to bend my legs and drape them over the edge. It wasn't particularly comfortable, but it would do.

I glanced at Asira, who stood with her arms crossed, modestly staring off into the forest instead of at my nakedness.

She had a beautiful home surrounded by trees, with a tiny barn in the back, chickens pecking around it. There was a path that snaked away, perhaps toward Terrin, or—I shivered—the boneyard, and she lived here alone. Did she have no fear?

“What do you want?” I asked.

Her arms tightened around her waist as her voice dipped. Staring off like that, the light caught her hair, and a slight wind blew back errant curls, giving me just a peek of her own pointed ears. Curious. Who exactly was my beautiful savior?

“I…I’m not sure. I grew up here, and I’ve lived well. I have a good job. I heal people, but...” she trailed off, and suddenly, her shoulders sloped in defeat. With a whirl, she faced me, eyes on my face but not meeting my gaze. “I want nothing. My life is fine as is. I’ll go make some food; you must be starving. Come inside when you’re done.”

Just like that, she spun on her heel, and a moment later, the door banged shut.

I tilted my head back, then submerged myself in the water. What a woman. What an attitude!

Slowly, as I lay there, an idea wormed its way through my mind, and try as I might, dangerous as it was, I wanted to enact it.

I was a Master, buried alive, and she was a mortal woman, a lonely mortal woman who didn’t know what she wanted. I had the power to change all that, and with that change, I'd enact my revenge.

# 3

## ASIRA

Drazhan returned with a towel wrapped around his waist. My face heated as his bulk filled the doorway, and once inside, my cottage felt much smaller as he filled it up with his presence.

A growing scene of unease came over me, and I pointed to the table where I'd placed a collection of clothes. "Something in that pile might fit you."

I felt his golden gaze on me as he shuffled through the clothes, but I turned my back on him so as not to see more of that tempting skin. Reason warred in my chest. He was one of the Masters, and I had no business looking at him with desire in my eyes. He resembled many things I did not have, including freedom and power.

Bending over the fire, I ladled a thick gruel into two bowls. When I turned around, he'd found some trousers. They settled low on his hips and were immodestly tight. He winked at me and settled into a chair, wincing as though something pained him. His wounds had to be internal because his flesh was without blemish.

I dusted his bowl with stardust and sat it in front of him. "Eat."

"As you command, my healer," he smirked.

I frowned, not appreciating his flirtatious tone, and I sat down as far away as possible from him. "How do you feel?"

He took a bite, froze, then swallowed hard.

The gruel.

Grandmother had despaired in teaching me to cook, but since I was good at mixing vials and using stardust, she taught me how to bargain. Often, in exchange for one of my tinctures or in payment for my work as a healer, the citizens of Terrin brought me food. They ensured I ate well. Otherwise, I made do with my own rudimentary skills.

"Better." He cleared his throat, finally answering my earlier question.

I bit back a laugh and glanced from the bowl to his face. "I put stardust in it. You have to eat it all."

One hand formed a fist, as though steeling himself for what was to come, and then he finished the bowl with lightning speed. With a self-indulgent smile, he set the empty bowl on the table and gestured to me. "What about you? Don't you need to keep up your strength?"

I scowled and swallowed another spoonful of the bland-tasting gruel. "As your healer, it is my duty to take care of you first. I assume your injuries are internal, so you should rest. Come."

Standing, I pulled back the curtain that divided the two rooms of the cottage. In the back was my room, a windowless section with space for a bed and a collection of treasures I stored underneath it. The woodcarver had made the bed, and I was rather proud of its size.

But now, staring at it, I stuck my tongue in my cheek. Drazhan was huge; he'd never fit.

Apparently, he agreed, for he hadn't budged from the table. "I will not sleep again, especially not during daylight. Let me help you while you work."

Inwardly fuming, I frowned. I'd hoped he'd sleep again so I could have the cottage to myself and work without him interrupting. He was distracting, and warmth skated through me each time I felt those intense golden eyes on me, which was often. Collecting stardust was my biggest job of the year, and I had long days of work before the tithe.

"Fine," I relented. "But you're healing. You're not supposed to do much. Sit in front of the fire and don't let it go out."

He spread his fingers. "Are you always this bossy?"

"I'm just telling you what I tell all who come to me for healing. If you don't rest, you'll make yourself worse."

"Do you give yourself the same advice?"

I wrinkled my nose in confusion. "Why?"

"I wager you slept little last night. Why don't you take a nap?"

My barking laugh cut him short, and I realized too late how rude I sounded. No one had looked out for my well-being since Grandmother passed, and his words nudged something in my soul. Was he trying to be kind, or did he have an alternative motive? "I'll rest when you rest," I said.

The morning passed.

Drazhan slouched in my rocking chair and dozed while I worked, spreading vials across the table and bottling stardust as best I could. I fell into a rhythm, completely forgetting about my guest, and jumped when his low voice rang out.

"When is the tithe?"

My body went rigid, and then I turned around, watching his long eyelashes sweep down. He appeared more alive than ever, and there was something in his tone, an urgency.

"In seven days. Why?"

His eyes glazed over, lost in thought. Holding up a hand, he counted with his fingers. "I recall spring, the flowers in full bloom, the gardens bright with life, then the confrontation, the stabbing. It's been six months since I was cast down."

My eyebrows shot up. "Six months?"

"Yes. I lay in the boneyard as if in death, and the stardust, no, I'm certain you, brought me back to life."

No, no, no. That couldn't be right. Stardust had healing properties, but it didn't bring anyone back to life. Still, six months was impossible. Whatever had happened to him had addled his mind. "I know what I want," I said, to distract him from his thoughts. Whatever he was thinking couldn't be good.

His golden gaze locked on mine. "What do you want?"

I wished I didn't feel breathless when he looked at me, as though he truly saw me, not just a healer but a lonely woman searching for more, something else to fulfill life and bring joy to the empty spaces within me. I blinked and spat out the words that had festered within me, unsaid, all along. "To be chosen."

As soon as the words left my mouth, I knew my request was wrong.

Every year, the Masters flew down from their floating kingdom in gilded chariots pulled by winged horses. They came to Terrin to collect a percentage of the grains, fruits, and vegetables grown by the farmers. They also took wild animals and livestock. All this was given to them in exchange for protecting us from the monsters beyond our land.

They also bestowed a far greater honor on Terrin, and citizens from far and wide came, hopeful, eager to be picked, for the chosen ones were taken back to the kingdom above and lived in grandeur and wealth. They were also never seen again, but it was a small price to pay, to leave everything behind to live in freedom and glory.

That was what I wanted: a change, an adventure, more than my humble life as the Stardust Collector.

It was a bold ask, because at twenty-eight, I was too old to be chosen.

Each year, the Masters choose five young women, usually between eighteen and twenty-one, and five young men. Somehow, they already knew who to pick, for they read from a scroll, calling the names of those who were chosen.

I'd seen the look on the faces of the chosen ones, eyes shining as they stepped forward to have their lives changed. I was never one of them, but he could make it so. Even disgraced, wasn't he still one of them?

Drazhan's eyes flashed, and he stood, casting a shadow, larger than life, across the room. For the first time, his voice was stern. "You don't want that."

I lifted my chin and crossed my arms, daring him. "Why not?"

"Something is wrong up there, with the Masters and their floating kingdom. I'm on a quest to find out what it is. I'm certain they tried to kill me because I found a clue. Once I discover the truth, I'm going to destroy them."

My jaw hung open, and I shook my head at his outrageous statement. Then, I burst into laughter. What a joke.

When I stopped, he was staring at me, something dark in his eyes. "You don't believe me, and why should you? I'll tell you my story and you can choose to believe it or not. I hold no influence over the tithe. Those who are chosen are meant to be chosen."

Drazhan resettled himself at the table. I crossed my arms, frustrated at his reaction to my wish. I expected him to dazzle me with tales of the kingdom in the sky, the chariots that floated across the clouds, and the Masters dressed in golden masks. They had banquets and feasts, dances and celebrations that rivaled even the gods, I was sure of it.

Drazhan didn't understand what it meant to be a commoner, to work until the skin of my hands cracked and bled, and my feet hurt so badly I had to limp. He didn't understand what it meant to be the Stardust Collector and walk into a creepy place to behold the glory above, glory I never got a taste of.

Each tithe left me with just a glimpse of how life could be different, easier. Not that I was complaining, but the opportunity to toil no more, to be dressed in royal garments with every need catered to, to live a life of indulgence instead of working myself to the bone, like my grandmother had done, was extremely compelling.

I'd been lucky enough to learn how to read the recipes for healing, but nothing more. I heard rumors of grand libraries in the floating kingdom, meat so succulent it melted in one's mouth, and the finest wines from vineyards far away.

He didn't understand because he'd come from that life, a Master born with everything at his fingertips. He lived a life of ease and pleasure, surrounded by beauty.

I didn't like the way he looked at me, as though he read my mind and sensed my vulnerabilities. My loneliness was getting the better of me, but I also knew if nothing changed, I'd live the exact same life my grandmother did, with no one to share it with or to pass the trade of Stardust Collector down to. Everything ended with me, so why not take a chance and change my life for the better?

Except, he was refusing after I'd saved and healed him.

A frown knit between my eyebrows, and I felt myself glaring at him, my voice hard and clipped as I said, "Please do. Explain yourself."

He tapped his long fingers lightly on the table, drawing attention to his short fingernails, chewed to the quick.

"I grew up in Hanadith, a city far from here, with twelve siblings. I was restless, anxious to prove myself, and so I joined the Sky Watch. The equivalent here in Terrin would be the knights, loyal to the Masters, but not allowed to enter the floating kingdom."

Despite my urge to be grumpy, I sat down and nodded. I knew about the knights, loyal to the floating kingdom. They were the men who ruled Terrin while the Masters sat in their lofty seats above, but even though the knights answered to the Masters, they were not invited into their kingdom. It left them with a sort of pining, a longing to dwell above when they were stuck down below.

Grandmother said the knights were strict and brutal because of it. I'd heard tales that made my blood curl of women who went out at night and then ended up at our doorstep nine months later, heavy with child, refusing to name a father. Any citizens caught for misdeeds by the knights were beaten bloody, even for minor misdemeanors.

I'd had an incident once when walking back from the market alone, and I shivered as I recalled it. One of the knights had attacked me, ripped my dress, and tried to force himself on me. Something dark had come over me, and I'd yanked my knife free and carved up his face. It was the only time I felt truly powerful, as though nothing could touch me.

After that, the knights pretended I did not exist, and when they needed help, they sent a young trainee to request supplies and offer me payment in the form of coins.

Drazhan continued, seemingly not noticing my internal battle. "I assumed the Sky Watch would be full of action, with monsters to shoot out of the sky and people to save. In reality, aside from training, there was very little to do, other than walk the walls of the keep. In order to prevent boredom and to entertain myself, I started sneaking out. I grew careless, and many followed my example, which led to a mutiny against those who led the Sky Watch. It could not have come at a worse time, for a great dragon attacked the city and burned it to the ground. We were so busy sparring amongst ourselves, we were not prepared when the time came to take up arms, kill a monster, and save the people. As the leader of the revolt, I was imprisoned, an outcast for years, until I was given a unique opportunity: death, or work for the Great Commissioner."

I rested my elbows on the table, whisked away by his tale of another land. I imagined the young men, all rowdy and dressed in armor, ready for battle, watching the skies for monsters. Then, I felt the sharp disappointment settling in their bellies as they realized the monsters weren't coming. There were no battles or wars, nothing but endless pacing and drills, waiting for something, anything, to happen.

I could relate to that, to the monotonousness of the everyday, waiting for something, *anything*, exciting to happen. "What is the Great Commissioner?" I asked.

"*Who* is the Great Commissioner," Drazhan corrected. "He oversees all, and he gave me a second chance to amend my mistakes. He sent me to the kingdom of High Terrin to find out what's wrong with the Masters and destroy them."

The dream shattered.

"You can't destroy the Masters," I protested. Holding up my hand, I ticked off reasons with my fingers. "They are at the very core of Terrin. They keep us alive, bless our crops, and protect us from the unnamed monsters who dwell beyond the clouds. If they are gone, Terrin cannot sustain itself."

"Terrin doesn't need the Masters to sustain itself. The people just need freedom and a good Stardust Collector."

# 4
# DRAZHAN

Asira's dark eyes flashed as she stared at me, a mix of disbelief and frustration crossing her face. Everything was clicking together now, and I wished I'd seen it before. All this time, I'd tried to work using my own strength, unwilling to seek help when the burden of guilt lay heavy on my shoulders.

It had been tempting to lose myself in the pleasures of the floating kingdom, but I was all too aware of the watching eye of the Great Commissioner. What would happen to me should I fail? In fact, hadn't I failed already and been given a second chance, along with a helper?

An insidious plan formed, risky and terrifying. My gaze flickered over the bottles of stardust. How many of them could I steal away without her noticing? More importantly, without *them* noticing? A wave of exhaustion overcame me. She was right; I needed rest and the conversation made my head hurt. "I'll take you up on the offer of that bed after all," I relented.

Her mouth went tight yet she nodded. "Go ahead, but this conversation isn't over."

I grinned at her. She was a woman who wanted something. Of course, this wasn't over. "As you wish. To be continued when I'm more awake."

My ribcage hurt as I stumbled to the room, velvet blackness overtaking me as I sank onto the bed. It was small, and whatever the mattress had been stuffed with was lumpy and poked at my back. How comfortable I'd been up in the floating kingdom, comfort and bliss at my fingertips, a bath I could actually fit in, delicious food. Was that what she was after?

From her perspective, the floating kingdom would be a dream come true, for that was how the Masters painted a picture of their kingdom. It was everything one could dream of or desire, coming together into one beautiful, perfect nirvana.

I shivered.

It was a world she did not belong in, but I could not sway her from her desires. It was a relief, at least, that I was not in charge of who was chosen, but she was right. I owed her for saving my life and introducing me to the power of stardust.

I WOKE SOMETIME LATER and pulled back the curtains, a chill washing over me. The fire had gone out, and the room was silent, black, as though thieves had come in the night and taken everything. Barefoot, I stepped into the main room, letting my eyes adjust.

Asira was slumped over the table, asleep. Bottles of stardust stretched from her fingertips across the table. How long had she worked before she collapsed? Loathe to wake her, I kneeled in front of the fireplace and stacked up wood, then whispered "*Elothe*. Burn."

The fire flickered to life, licking at the wood, slowly then eagerly. Burning. Burning. Burning.

I closed my eyes against the reminder of burning flesh and screams. It had been a mistake, all one, terrible mistake.

The door was ajar, and I slipped outside, noticing the empty wheelbarrow and jars scattered around the front door. A glimmer of stardust sparkled in those empty vessels, but nothing more. I walked through the trees – I needed meat.

It had been a while since I'd been on the earth, and walking barefoot across the cold ground gave me time to think. What, exactly, had happened up in High Terrin?

Try as I might, I couldn't recall what the clue was, nor who'd discovered my identity. Once healed, I had to find answers, but for now, it was peaceful to walk the land again with no agenda and enjoy the company of someone beautiful and smart, someone who did not wear a mask and pretend to be someone she was not.

Asira didn't believe me, and how could I fault her? My own memories were shaky, just a strong sense that something was wrong. Part of me was tempted to return and take her with me. She could help with my investigation and get a taste of the glory of that haunted kingdom. After the tithe, I'd return, find out what had happened, and, if it was safe, bring her along with me. Six months was a long time, and with a disguise, I could easily blend back in without mishap.

Sucking in a cold breath of air, I lifted my face to the sky where a quilt of stars watched me like a thousand eyes. The dark shapes of the three floating islands blocked out portions of the sky, and I shuddered, unable to shake my suspicion.

Nowhere was safe, especially not up there.

# 5
## ASIRA

Drazhan was gone.

The curtain was open, displaying my empty bed. The fire had burned out, the sun was up, and he was gone. I waited, a twist of fury and disappointment gathering. I was at the peak of my life changing and, without any regard for my request, he'd bolted.

What did I expect?

The Masters were above all mortals, both literally and metaphorically. They were better than the humans of Terrin in every way: physically taller and stronger, their minds smarter and more innovative, and they had a secret weapon. It was only spoken about in hushed tones, but many said they had magic.

I only knew because Grandmother told me tales about the Masters, how they came to bring balance to the land and watch over the people, not only protecting them from wild monsters, but from raiders and nomads and invading barbarians. The Masters controlled the weather and caused the crops to grow, made the pastures abundant for the grazing animals, and gave us peace to build buildings, expand our livelihoods, and raise families.

The Masters lived above us like gods, but Grandmother said there was another reason, a deeper, forgotten reason. They had an aversion to iron. It weakened them and kept them from tapping into the source of their magic.

I stilled, my fingers running over a bottle of stardust. Drazhan had made some claims about the Masters. What if...

I let the thought hang there for a second, then shook it off and got to work. He'd gone, and it was best I put all of it out of my mind instead of speculating. He had to be mistaken.

The door banged open.

I snatched a knife from the table and whirled to face the intruder.

Drazhan leaned against the doorframe, still maddeningly shirtless but grinning at me, something furry in one hand. "I was hoping you'd have a knife. May I borrow it?"

I hated how sweet relief swept through me – I shouldn't be happy to see him. Trying to hide my expression, I pointed to what he held. "Depends on what you're using the knife for. What is that?"

"A rabbit. Figured you cooked a meal for me, so it's my turn to cook for you."

My eyes went wide. "Eating the wildlife is forbidden. Surely, you know this."

"I'm well aware of that law, but what's the fun in following the rules?"

"You're going to get me into trouble."

He smirked. "On the contrary. I'm going to give you a meal you won't forget."

"I'm supposed to be the one helping you."

Drazhan stretched and gave me a devious wink. "You are. I already feel like myself again, and I want to eat real food, meat. One cannot thrive on stardust alone, and I dare say, you need to rest. Did you sleep on the table all night?"

Oh. My hand went to my face. I hadn't done my hair at all, just sat up and started working. I was still wearing the same dress I'd been wearing for two, or was it three days in a row now? It was wrinkled and stained, and I must smell a bit. "I...I have work to do!"

"I can see that, but it appears you're almost done, and a break never hurt anyone. Why don't you take a bath while I make a meal as a thank you? You've been very kind."

*Kind.* My heart beat faster and a lightning bolt of heat crawled up my spine. I scowled. "It is my duty."

"You're not very agreeable, are you? Take the compliment and stop deflecting. You won't change my mind."

With a huff, I snatched up a dress and bag of herbs, hating to admit he was right. Instead of getting lost in my work, I needed to take care of myself. Striding to the door, I held out the knife, handle first, giving him my most serious look. “Don’t get any ideas.”

He laughed and pressed a hand to his heart, those golden eyes twinkling. “I dare not invoke your wrath, nor risk the curse you might put on me.”

I bit back a laugh as his hand closed around mine, his long fingers stroking the inside of my wrist. My silly giggle turned into a staggered breath as a tingling sensation went up my spine. Snatching my hand away, I hurried around the cottage, heat flaming across my face.

I tried not to think about him as I washed, scrubbing the dirt and stardust off my skin.

I tried not to think about the way his golden eyes twinkled, or the fact that I enjoyed sparring words with him.

I tried not to think about the fact that he was the first man who’d looked at me, truly looked at me, in years.

A sob built in my throat, and I bit it back. My loneliness was getting the best of me. Perhaps that’s just how the Masters were outside their masks. I still needed a boon from him before he left for good. That's what I'd focus on.

# 6
# DRAZHAN

By the time Asira returned, the meat was fully cooked, juices dripping into the fire. She strode in, bringing the scent of wood with her. A basket of greenery was tucked under one arm, and her hair was loose, falling about her shoulders and softening her features. The baggy dress she wore did her no favors, but I thought her beautiful, a forest fairy who saved me.

A fleeting vision overcame me, of gathering her in my arms and burying my nose in her hair, inhaling her scent until it was painted in my memory. How was it that a woman like her had no husband? No, it was more likely she'd flat-out refused any who'd asked.

"Marry me," I whispered under my breath.

Those sharp brown eyes flashed in my direction, then narrowed. Her nose quivered as she sniffed the air, then relented. "It smells good."

"It will be the best meal you've ever had," I boasted. Asira grunted and moved toward the fire, but I pointed to the table. "Sit. It's my turn to serve you."

"I don't need to be served," she protested, but she sat down all the same.

"True," I agreed as I dished up the meat, along with some root vegetables I'd found while poking through her cottage. "But my desire to serve you is out of honor, not because I see any weakness in you."

She tilted her head, looking up at me from under her long eyelashes as I slid the plate in front of her. "I think it's because you're too trusting."

Now, it was my turn to snort. I moved to sit at the opposite head of the table, and then, at the last moment, I pivoted and sat down to the right of her. Elbows on the table, she frowned at my closeness, eliciting a bit of glee. "If only you knew. But I've made up my mind about you."

"Have you?" Asira muttered, spearing a piece of meat with her fork. She bit into it, and her entire face changed. Her shoulders relaxed, a light crept into her eyes, and she groaned. "This is delicious. It melts in my mouth. How is that possible?"

"I made it."

"So, the tales are true. Masters have magic."

Magic.

The bite of that word threatened to ruin my good mood. Instead, I enjoyed the savory taste of an actual meal before responding. "Masters aren't mortal, which is why they give off a mystical aura, and many assume it is because of magic. You, however, are refreshing, and although I don't know you well, I get a sense of your demeanor already. You enjoy your space and privacy while priding yourself on a job well done. As a healer, you have skills that allow you to take care of yourself, and you don't need anyone's help, although it would be wise for you to have an assistant, at least during the time of year when you collect stardust. You are strong on your own, unafraid, and you don't want help, because that would mean owing someone, and you absolutely do not accept charity. Except for a meal now and then, because you can't cook. You aren't married because it's a sign of settling down, but you want more than what life offers down here, and that's why you want to be chosen."

A strained silence followed my gleeful pronouncement, and then Asira put down her fork, voice cold. "I did not ask you to read my fortune, but if this is your way of ensuring I will be chosen, I will accept it."

I wished she was not so focused on being chosen. With a sigh, I rubbed my temples, doubting my plan to take her with me. "I am one of the Masters, and I owe you for saving my life, but, as I've said before, I have no control over who is chosen. What will be, will be. If it's change or an adventure you desire, I will ensure you have it. I must admit, while I have a task to do, it's peaceful here with you, and I believe you would benefit from kisses."

The corner of her mouth quirked up, but she calmly finished her plate, before resting her elbows on the table and leaning closer to me. "I've never figured out why people are so interested in the fact that I'm not married. They should mind their own business, and that includes you. As for kisses, you're not the first one to propose a kiss as a fair payment, and I assure you it is not, since it would benefit you more than it would benefit me."

This was unexpected, but her calmness enticed me. I leaned closer, inhaling her intoxicating scent. "How would you know who it benefits if you've never tried?"

Asira stood up rather suddenly, swiping the plates off the table. "Thank you for dinner. It was delicious, but I find the conversation lacking."

Ah. So, my words had struck a nerve. I grinned as she marched away from me and called out. "I will stay until the tithe, and then I will leave you in peace. Will you endure my presence until then?"

"If I must."

I resisted the urge to fold her into my arms and kiss that petulant mouth. It would only earn me a slap, for she was determined to have her way.

Still, a stray thought wormed its way through my mind: what if, by some miracle, she *was* chosen?

# 7
## ASIRA

The morning of the tithe dawned in a haze of pale pink, the air tinged with the crisp hint of winter. I was up before the sun fully rose, my fingers trembling with anticipation as I tightened my cloak around me. When I lifted the curtain and stepped into the main room, a gust breezed into the room. The door was open, and Drazhan stood in the doorway, shirtless as always, watching the shadows fade under the impending rays of dawn.

At last.

He'd leave, and I'd resume the normality of my daily life, except that's not what I wanted. Was it possible that even without his blessing, I'd be chosen?

"I'm leaving today," Drazhan announced without turning around, an odd note in his voice.

I swallowed my retort.

He continued. "Will you be fine without me?"

"Why wouldn't I be?"

He faced me. "A red dawn spells foul omens for all."

I didn't like this side of him, for his warnings left me with the sense that the future held something menacing. "Will you not relent and allow me to become one of the chosen?"

He frowned, a deep disappointment in his tone when he spoke. "Asira, I've told you, the Masters are not the kind gods you believe in. Going to their kingdom will be your undoing, and I will have no part in it, especially after what you've done for me. If, by some miraculous reason, you are chosen, you must stay calm and never, ever eat or drink anything they give you."

I grimaced. "Why not?"

All the mischief was gone from Drazhan's face as he approached me, tangling his fingers in my curls he tilted my head up. In stunned surprise, I had no recourse but to stare at him. Why did my chest feel tight, and my breath come so fast? I wanted nothing to do with this immortal Master, and yet he was so close, I smelled the headiness of his scent, masculine and woody.

Drazhan's assumption about my lack of a husband had been correct.

A few shy lads had asked, and I'd scorned them by tossing their words back in their faces.

Marriage. Why?

To be burdened with a man, forced to have his babies, provide food for his belly, and keep the cottage respectable? I'd end up working myself to the bone all for a union I cared nothing for.

Throughout the seven days Drazhan had spent with me, he asked for nothing. In fact, he was helpful, keen on ensuring I didn't work too hard. I hadn't been lonely at all, and he'd given me a glimpse of what it would be like to have a relationship that benefited both of us.

"Hear me, Asira," he said, voice low and dangerous. "You will not be chosen for the tithe, and I have unfinished business in the floating kingdom above. I vow that when I am done, I will return to you and ensure you have what your heart desires."

Then, he kissed me.

I assumed I knew what it meant to be kissed: wet, sloppy lips against mine that I'd wipe away in disgust, or a bloom of terrible breath clouding my senses.

Drazhan's kiss was none of those.

His lips were firm, and underneath his masculine scent was the tang of stardust and magic.

A tingling rushed through my lower belly, and my arms went slack, as though my entire body would melt into him.

My lips parted, tasting him, welcoming his caress.

*This* was what kissing felt like?

No wonder. I parted my lips for more, wanting to drown myself in the moment, but Drazhan pulled back before I could fully reciprocate, his golden eyes blazing with...need?

He brushed his thumb over my lips, and awareness flooded my body. “I have wanted to kiss you since the day I met you.”

I couldn’t have responded even if I’d known what words to say. Something had happened to me. I couldn’t think or breathe; in fact, my entire body felt boneless.

The corner of Drazhan’s mouth quirked up, and suddenly, he was at the door again. “Farewell, Asira. We shall meet again.”

Just as suddenly as he’d appeared in my life, he was gone.

I stood frozen in shock just a moment longer, then lifted my shaking fingers to my mouth and wiped his kiss away. It meant nothing, and I would not think about the kiss or the fact that he’d left without giving me a boon for healing him.

Giving myself a shake, I tugged on my boots, slammed the door, and followed the trail through the woods to the ceremony.

TITHE WAS A HIGHLY anticipated celebration as people from across Terrin poured into the city. In the center rose a bedrock of marble, rich with carvings, and a platform where the Masters parked their golden chariots.

The marble mountain also served as a barrier between Terrin and the wild lands where nomads and barbarians dwelled, raiding and pillaging. These were the people the Masters protected Terrin from, as well as from monsters and other creatures that lurked in the dark, ready to drag the weak and helpless away from their homes.

Legend held that before the Masters came, women and children being stolen away was a common occurrence. Not so anymore.

The crowd had already gathered by the time I arrived. A buzz of excitement swept through those gathered as bodies pressed close together, eager to see and hear from the Masters. I paused on a swell of land, almost too far back for a good view. I should have left before sunrise in order to get close to the marble steps. It was known that the Masters never set foot on our land, and today was the first day I wondered why.

Curse Drazhan and his unsettling rumors. I'd never questioned the actions of the Masters before. Why today?

Pushing the thought out of my head, I turned my gaze skyward as trumpets sounded. A few moments later, winking spots of light appeared from the floating kingdom, growing bigger as they neared land.

Ten golden chariots, pulled by winged horses, flew through the air and landed on the marble platform. A bloom of awe warmed my body, and I clasped my hands together as the crowd cheered.

Motes of silver sprang out as the horses tucked away their wings and the Masters dismounted, tall, ethereal beings dressed in white robes, with straight locks of golden hair to their waists and gilded masks covering their faces. They moved with grace and power, and a yearning filled me, aching to be close to them. My fingers tingled, and a lump swelled in my throat.

"Please, let me be chosen," I whispered. "This is what I want."

The ceremony began with a speech. One of the masked Masters stepped forward and spoke, but what he said was so familiar, my mind wandered. The Masters always shared about the dangers they faced, driving the monsters away and keeping the land bountiful. Then came the great invitation.

I straightened my shoulders, waiting, listening breathlessly as they called the names of five young men. They always chose the men first, then the women.

The call was viewed as a great honor bestowed upon the families of the chosen. I tried to kick Drazhan's words out of my mind and reminded myself that the chosen were being blessed. They'd get the opportunity to live in wealth and glory among the Masters.

After the men were called, they went to the platform and were welcomed onto the golden chariots. Three of them raced away without waiting for the women.

The Master cleared his throat, unfurled his second scroll, and began to call names, one by one.

Sari, daughter of Beth the weaver.

Bridget, daughter of Brigetta the tailer.

Asira, daughter of Sira, The Stardust Collector.

Lightheadedness made my vision swim, and my knees went weak. I didn't hear the rest of his words nor the final two names called.

I'd been chosen!

Hands touched my arms and back, pushing me toward the marble mountain, congratulating me.

Numbly, I walked up the stairs to join the other chosen, my ears ringing.

Perhaps Drazhan had been good luck after all.

# 8
## DRAZHAN

During the tithe was the best time to sneak into the floating kingdom, because all eyes were on the Masters, and no one was staring up at the floating islands.

After I left Asira's cottage, I went to the boneyard and gave a long, low whistle.

As soon as I did, a beast flew out of the sky, a strange bird called Egon that appeared like a cross between an eagle and a dragon. Egon was a wild beast, but I'd made friends with him in anticipation of a time when I'd need to return to the floating islands without the aid of a chariot.

When I'd been in the Sky Watch, I had a great eagle to ride into battle, and Egon reminded me of that beast.

I tossed myself onto the hard scales of Egon's back before he got too interested in the gruesome sight of white bones spread beneath the leafy boughs. As we flew, another memory bloomed, and I recalled the name of the Master responsible for trying to kill me: Iscariot.

An icy shiver went through me as I recalled the blade in my side. The warning made me want to turn away instead of returning to the kingdom of grace and glory.

At least this time, I had someone to return to in Terrin.

Asira.

Unless the kiss scared her off and she ran away. That was an entirely possible situation, and the idea of hunting her down entertained me.

It would be wise to forget about being entangled with a mortal, although I recalled the pointed ears she kept hidden. Spending a week with her didn't give me the chance to find out more about her, apart from the fact that she was raised by her grandmother, who groomed her to become the next Stardust Collector.

I waffled with the idea of returning for her after the tithe. Wasn't it risky to put someone I cared about in danger, especially when my memories were still unclear?

The largest island rose before me, and I balanced on Egon's back and leaped. I rolled onto peat moss, the impact knocking my breath from my lungs, but I forced myself to keep moving, rasping as I crawled to the marble statues.

The Masters were fond of carving their likeness into statues, or at least the version of themselves wearing their golden hair—I recalled those were wigs—and the carved masks that hid their faces and eyes.

Statues dotted the three floating islands, and as I walked, I recalled each statue held a secret. Was that the clue I'd discovered? No, who would stab me for learning the entrance to the network of tunnels underground?

I reached the first statue, unlocked a trap door, and closed it behind me. As I made my way into the tunnels, memories flashed before me: running, screams, blood, a roar of anger, the stink of decay, and red. So much red.

A chill passed over me, and goosebumps pebbled on my arms. A warning. But I couldn't flee. The tunnels were where I'd crept in secret, spying and searching for the truth. It was also where I stored my clothes and weapons. Today, I had a jar of stardust to add to my collection.

Finding my stash, I dressed, pulling on the robe, my golden hair, and that horrible, restrictive, gilded mask. It had a symbol on it noting my identity, which was risky to wear in a place where I was supposed to be dead. Why hadn't I been wearing the mask when I'd fallen?

During the past six months, no one had found my things. Had I taken a risk and gone out unmasked? A sense warned me that it was forbidden to walk the halls of the floating kingdom without a mask, at least for the Masters. Frowning, I tucked away the stardust and tugged on a vial to hang around my neck. Tucking my knife into the band of my robe, I set off for the exit.

Rumor had it that because of their magic, the Masters were susceptible to iron, a rumor I knew to be false. There was something that the Masters could not tolerate, and I sensed I had found it and planned on using it to discover the truth. That revelation still escaped me, and I had to be careful as I sought out Iscariot for revenge.

I crept through the tunnels and took the ladder that led to the kitchens, ignoring the foul tang that hung in the air. After a while, I'd grown used to the odd scent, yet it still threatened to turn my stomach.

My fingertips touched the walls, the familiarity of the place growing stronger. I recalled the twists and turns, the passageways that led nowhere, the twists that made no sense, and the secret entrance I couldn't find. Because of the tithe, the halls were silent, only hushed whispers spoken. Most must be at the great hall, preparing for the ceremony. What if I was too late?

At last, I reached the hall of chambers where the Masters dwelled. Double doors were closed, and on each one was carved a rune that matched the ones on their masks. I paused outside of Iscariot's chambers, frightening memories surfacing, but it wasn't enough. I placed my hand on the knob, envisioning the truth on the other side. If he'd already gone to the great hall, I could at least search his chambers for clues.

Opening the door, I slipped inside and took off my mask.

Iscariot's chambers were vast and rich, three connected rooms with tapestries and carpets, mirrors and crystals, clothing made of the finest silk, and a mask for every day. I closed the door behind me, my hand going to my knife as a voice drawled from the other side of the wall. "Is that you, Jabel? You're too early, go away."

"It's not Jabel," I said, "and you run the risk of being late to the ceremony."

Iscariot snorted. "As if I'd miss my own mating ceremony."

I stilled. Iscariot's time had come, and he was to mate with one of the chosen today. A marriage, if one could call it that. If he went missing, the incident would be far too noticeable, and I feared what retaliation the Masters would take.

Iscariot chose that moment to come around the corner and enter the main sitting room. He was half-dressed, mask on, golden hair shining, but he paused, staring at my naked face. “Oh. You. I could have sworn I killed you the first time.”

I held up my blade. “A mistake you’ll regret, because you won’t get a chance to kill me again.”

Iscariot stepped toward me, unafraid. “You forget, I know who you truly are, and I warned the Masters about you. You’re not one of us, you infiltrating spy. You seek to undo all the right we’ve done for centuries.”

“I seek to free Terrin from your masquerade.”

“What is done cannot be undone. We are too strong, too powerful.”

I laughed. “With one flaw. I know your weakness: your race is dying out.”

“You forgot about the tithe; one of the women will be the answer. In fact, this year, we changed the requirements and focused on families with a little magic in their bloodlines.”

“Mortals don’t have magic,” I countered.

"Oh Drazhan, you pretend to be so wise. If only you knew." Iscariot shook his head, and then he leaped.

He hurled into me, and I slammed against the back wall, causing the room to shake.

Roaring, I brought up my fist and punched him in the stomach. He retaliated with a blow to my face. I ducked, his fist catching the top of my head, rocking me back.

I fumbled for the knife as a blow landed on my shoulder. Throwing an elbow, I caught him in the chest, and he staggered back, giving me time to pull my knife.

I should have had it in hand before I walked into the room. My reflexes were too slow.

Iscariot gave a barking laugh and brought up his fists, hurling toward me again as I drove the knife up.

He froze as black blood poured from his side, and when he spoke, his voice was a low hiss. "You'll have to do better if you intend on killing me."

Then, he leaped on top of me. I went down hard, the knife flying out of my hands as claws tore at my clothing. My hands went up to defend my face, and I yanked Iscariot's mask off. He growled as one of his claws nicked the leather string that held the vial of stardust.

In the struggle, the top came off, and it fell, shattering on the floor and sending a cloud of dust into the air.

Iscariot howled and hurled himself back, hissing.

Interesting.

Leaping to my feet, I snatched up the stardust and threw it in his face then dove for my knife.

A burning stench filled the air as claws ripped my robe. I grunted, ran my knife across his throat, and stabbed him through the heart.

Iscariot slumped to the floor, twitching, burning.

Breathing heavily, I stood over him, grimacing at his true appearance.

Memories came rushing back. Iscariot had caught me off guard outside of the palace. I hadn't my knife or the mask that helped me blend in. He'd been stalking me as I'd stalked him.

A pounding came on the door. "It's time!"

"One moment," I shouted back. The ceremony!

My eyes tore around the room, searching for a place to hide the body.

Under the bed would do until I returned. I only hoped no one would notice the smell or the blood stains.

I tugged a rich carpet over the blood and snatched up Iscariot's mask, giving myself a fleeting glimpse in the mirror.

The pounding came again. "Hurry up, Iscariot. We can't be late."

I flung open the door. "I'm ready."

# 9
## ASIRA

My name. At last, they had called my name.

Emotion surged through me: joy, disbelief, and then...disquiet.

Words I'd forgotten floated back to my mind.

*"One day, Grandmother, when I grow up, I want to be chosen, like the beautiful girls at tithe. They get to fly away in golden chariots and live in the starry kingdom. It must be magnificent. I bet they are treated like princesses."*

*Grandmother sat up straight, dark eyes clouding over as she stared at me. A trembling hand fell from the mixture she'd been stirring to the table as she pressed her lips together. "Oh, my lovely Asira, what a dream you have.*

*The fates will do what they wish, but you have a unique task here as the next Stardust Collector. When I'm gone, you must carry on."*

*I'd been fifteen then, and those words were not what I wanted to hear. "I don't understand. You won't even let me collect stardust with you. What if I want to do something else?"*

*Grandmother shook her head firmly. "You can't. Your future is already set. I suppose it's time I told you. Why do you think I always have you hide your ears?"*

*"I don't know."*

*"It's because you have fae blood, child, and your pointed ears would give away your identity."*

*My fingers went to my curls, hiding the shape of my ears. "Why? Is there something wrong with my ears? With being part fae? Everyone likes us."*

*"Of course they do, because we are the healers, and our fae blood has given us that power. But once, long ago, the Masters warred with the fae and cast them out. That's why you don't see any fae around here. This land belongs to the Masters, and it is best we do our duty and avoid drawing attention to ourselves. Perhaps they have forgotten their old enemy, but what if they haven't? Stay*

*away from them and dreams of living in their kingdom. It's difficult to hide your true self from those you dwell with."*

THE MEMORY FADED, as did the reminder of the fear that gripped my heart back then. Nothing had come of it, and no one else knew the legends of a war between the Masters and fae. Besides, the Masters wore masks; how difficult would it be to hide my ears as I did daily?

In the floating kingdom, I'd finally be able to find answers, about the war and perhaps what had happened to my parents. They left one day for a journey they'd never returned from. I'd always imagined they were stolen away, perhaps by the Masters.

Forcing myself back to the present moment, I blinked and came to a standstill on the marble platform, inches from those golden chariots. Up close, they were even more impressive, the horses standing six hands high, white and silver feathers gracing their wings. I ached to reach out and touch them, still finding it difficult to believe my luck. Within moments, I'd be whisked away to the floating islands to live in a dreamland, surrounded by gold and glory.

The platform was crowded, full of the other woman who'd been chosen. It always went this way. First, the young men were taken, then the young women. Finally, the final wave of Masters took the offerings, food, and animals, and we were left in silence for another year.

Usually, this was the time I turned away and made my way back to home. Alone. Today, as the applause from the crowd came and the young women waved goodbye, I studied the Masters.

They glided along the platform wearing fine robes that swept to their booted feet, made of the finest thread and woven with silver and gold. Their hair – was it possible that *was* their hair? It was all golden and silky, while their masks were covered in an assortment of jewels, each one creating a distinct symbol. That must be how they distinguished themselves while dressed up.

We always saw them in robes and masks, and I wondered if they wore them daily. The garb was because we were not worthy to look upon their faces, but I'd seen Drazhan's face and hadn't died.

My lips burned, and my heart kicked at the memory of him. I wondered if he were above right now, and what I'd do if...no *when* I ran into him again. Would he be pleased to see I'd found my way to the floating islands after all?

A touch at my back broke me out of my thoughts. A white-gloved hand waved, and a low male voice said, "Please, to the chariots."

I had many questions, but my tongue swelled in my mouth, excitement and disbelief rendering me speechless. Following him—or her, the mask and the billowing robe made it impossible to tell—I stepped onto the chariot.

"Hold on," the Master said, arms on either side of me.

The smooth edges of the chariot shone blindingly bright, and I blinked against the light and held on to the railing. The reins were lifted, and a shrill whistle sounded.

Wings spread and with a jolt, we were up and off into the air. My ears rang and my belly dropped to my toes as we ascended. Wind tore at my hair, tugging it loose from my messy braid and whipping it around my face. The light intensified, making my eyes hurt. Bile churned in my stomach, and my limbs felt boneless. I sagged against the Master, willing myself not to heave on my first flight.

Up and up we went, whirling across beams of sunlight. The horse floated, wings spread wide, and the roiling in my belly stopped as the ride became smooth.

Fluffy white clouds floated almost close enough to reach up and touch, and the sky stretched endlessly in all directions, displaying hues of blue I'd never imagined. Even though I'd worn my warm cloak, cold air whipped through my clothes, a chill settling in my bones. I blinked wetness out of my eyes, not daring to let go of the chariot as the clouds parted, revealing the three floating islands.

I gasped.

They were much bigger than I'd imagined. From down below, I only glimpsed a triangle of brown dirt and gray rock. Occasionally, the mists that hovered underneath the islands would clear, displaying a glimmer from above, and when one stood on a high hilltop, one might make out pointed towers.

Now, my jaw dropped as I took in the rolling hills, vibrant gardens, and glistening waterfalls. Unlike Terrin, the land wasn't barren, readying itself for winter, but appeared like a summer day.

Trees sprung out of the ground, some of them in thick groves, but what drew my attention was the palace. It sat perched on the largest floating island, turrets pointing to the sky like fingers, towers glistening white and gold. Yet, there was darkness to it I could not describe.

We flew directly to the front of the palace and landed on a green lawn. My ears rang as I stepped off the chariot on unsteady feet. The ground beneath me was lush, the dirt rich with color. The scent of summer surrounded me, as though the floating kingdom were frozen in time. Only the bite in the air warned me of the coming winter, but I was grateful for the cold air that cleared my head.

The other women had landed and spun in small circles as they took our surroundings. Their faces glowed with anticipation, and they waved at me, as though we were friends. I waved back, feeling a buzzing sense of joy.

The horses and chariots were led away, and Masters surrounded us. Steps led up to marble columns that framed the palace doors. One of the Masters stood in front of those open doors, surrounded by masked others. Some of them were male, but others were female, wearing dresses and masks that only hid their eyes, not their entire faces. Did that mean the masks were only for the ceremony and not every day?

"Welcome to High Terrin," the Master standing in the middle boomed, his deep voice resounding with authority. "You are the blessed ones, and we are honored to welcome you here. In a moment, you will enter the palace and strip away all your raiment from Terrin, symbolic of your old life being stripped away as you enter your new life. Nothing from down below may enter here. Once you are dressed in your new raiment, the ceremony to celebrate your arrival shall begin, where we will bestow upon you our highest honor. I'm sure many of you have questions, which shall be answered in due time. For now, relax, enjoy the celebration, and again, welcome to High Terrin."

I clasped my hands together, still finding it hard to believe this was actually happening. Everything felt surreal, like a dream, the sun a bit too bright, the air a bit too cold, and the glitter of gold a bit too harsh on my eyes. Regardless, I followed the Masters up the shimmering steps, eager to see the inside of the palace.

But I did not get far.

One of the masked females took my hand and guided me into a large room. A fire roared in the hearth, which took up one wall, and white robes hung in a line. I turned, seeing that the other young women from Terrin were with me.

I'd been warned, but I was still stunned when one of the masked females took my cloak from around my shoulders and tossed it into the fire. My chest squeezed at the waste, and then I saw they were doing the same to the others, throwing away their clothing from Terrin, undoing their braids and brushing their hair.

One of the women, Sari I thought, let out a squeal as a necklace was snatched from her neck. She lunged for it. "Please! Not that."

A slap came, loud and striking. Sari stepped back, hand to her face as one of the fully-masked Masters stepped away. He snatched the necklace and tossed it in the fire. "Nothing from down below remains here."

I wrapped my hands around my bare shoulders, suddenly disconcerted not only with how he'd treated Sari, but that he was in the room while the females dressed us. With his mask, it was impossible to tell if he was staring at our naked bodies or not.

Regardless, I turned my back to him as the masked female assisting me pulled a white gown over my head. It was simple and fell to my ankles, the material no different from my clothes in Terrin; in fact, it was slightly scratchy. Disappointing. I expected the richest silks. The dress, like the robes the Masters wore, hung loosely on my body. Would I be expected to wear this every day?

I glanced again at Sari, whose eyes were glassy, unfocused, as her hair was brushed. A niggling went down my spine. What, exactly, did the Masters want with us in their kingdom? I'd always assumed it was for some noble reason, some high honor...but now?

Once we were dressed, our hair hanging down our backs, the masked females ushered us out of the room, and we followed one of the Masters deeper into the palace.

I titled my head back, taking in the tall, white columns and the crisscross of patterns covering them. Floor-to-ceiling windows let in an abundance of light, many of the panes painted in various colors, forming pictures. I strained to see them but eventually gave up, for it was impossible to see everything.

Rich carpets covered the stone floor, warm against my now-bare feet. Crystals hung from the ceiling, and when the windows disappeared, carved statues took their place.

All too quickly, we came to a stop. The masked females flitted away, leaving myself and the four other women standing at the top of a flight of stairs in front of an audience, perhaps the entire assembly of Masters.

Dumbly, I stared down at the stairs. Instead of leading into the hall where the Masters waited, the stairs led into a pool of water, dividing us from the Masters.

The Master had mentioned the ceremony, but I didn't believe he'd actually have us bathe in front of everyone. Suddenly, I understood the simpleness of the gown. Still, it was unnerving to have hundreds of golden masks pointed in my direction, the Masters watching, their emotions hidden.

My arms trembled, and I thought of Drazhan's words and my grandmother's warning about fae and Masters. An eerie sense of foreboding came over me, and I sniffed.

An odd tang hung in the air. It was a distinct odor, similar to the scent of a festering wound. Yet it was only an undercurrent, for most of the air was perfumed with a lilac scent.

I pinched my thigh. My nerves were making me imagine things when I needed to focus on the honor being bestowed upon myself and the other women. I didn't see any sign of the young men – were they not part of the ceremony?

A low chant began, and one of the Masters moved to a corner, where a jug and goblets sat. He poured five goblets and handed each of us one, murmuring, "May your spirits be renewed as you drink."

The goblet was heavy in my hands, and the drink looked like dark red wine. I paused, Drazhan's words ringing in my ears.

*Never, ever eat or drink anything they give you.*

Why? What could be so wrong with a drink?

Noticing my hesitation, the Master paused before me, tipping the goblet toward my lips. "Drink," he encouraged.

This was my new life; I should face it without fear.

I put the goblet to my lips and drank. Deeply.

It tasted like wine, except sweeter than any kind I'd ever had. Then, the aftertaste rang back, bold, deep, and bitter.

My lips tingled, and then my fingers and toes. A few moments passed, and then a sense of euphoria came over me, as though I were floating, and a haze of gold appeared in front of me.

Dimly, I heard the instructions of the Masters.

"Go down the steps, enter the water, and walk out the other side, clean and ready for your mate."

Mate. Funny, they used that word as though I was about to be married.

Indeed, soon came the music, and I moved as though I were in a dream, down into the water, watching as it rendered my dress completely sheer. I lifted a hand and moved my sleeve, feeling as though I were outside of my body, hovering above it, watching but not actively participating.

More mummers came, and then I was walking out of the pool, up the stairs. Water poured off me onto the floor, and I slipped on the wet hem of my robe.

One of those golden-masked Masters caught me around the waist and pressed me against his hard body. My dress soaked the front of his robe, and I wrapped my hands around his arms to steady myself. Whatever was in that drink made me feel woozy.

He bent his golden hair near mine and when he spoke, I knew that voice. "Oh Asira, what have you done?"

# 10

## DRAZHAN

Asira giggled as I carried her back to Iscariot's room, the drug already working through her system. I'd forgotten about the ceremony, the mating, and the drug worked into the wine that took away fear, making the humans more malleable when they arrived in High Terrin.

It was disconcerting, the way the Masters always wore their masks and used routine rituals to guide their days. I held Asira close, fighting between fear and fury. How had she been chosen, and what if I hadn't been there to take Iscariot's place? She would have been mated to *him*.

There were many things I needed to tell her, but she had to be sober. The drug would last for at least a few hours, although sweating it out of her system in a hot bath might speed up her recovery. She was the healer; she should be able to tell me what to do, despite her inebriated state.

I had to admit, I liked the way she held on to me, all her restraints gone. I suspected she had some sort of attraction toward me, but when I'd kissed her, she'd frozen, more stunned than anything else. Instead of giving her a chance to reciprocate, I'd left before she rejected me.

I studied the symbols on the doorway as I passed. Behind me, the Masters were returning to their chambers amid laughter and cheers. Rounds of wine had been passed around, and I was certain the women from Terrin weren't the only ones who'd soon be out of their minds. First was the ceremony, and then, seven days later, a great banquet was held. I'd been at that banquet once, a year ago, and it was the first time I sensed something was terribly wrong.

It was frustrating, how I was no closer to the truth than I'd been a year ago, and the clue I'd discovered remained locked in my returning memory. That, or it hadn't been as powerful as I recalled. Why hadn't I interrogated Iscariot before killing him?

I banged open the door, a half-moon with three stars above the doorframe confirming it was Iscariot's room. Someone had come to clean up: the clothing had been rearranged, and trays of food sat in the main sitting area. A vase of red flowers was perched near the trays, but the floral scent failed to completely cover up the old tang of blood and iron. I stiffened and dropped Asira into a chair. Pointing a finger at her, I said, "Stay there," and peeked my head into the bedroom.

It was undisturbed. I'd hidden the body under the bed and dragged a rug over the blood. I was safe. For now.

Removing my mask, I studied the room again. Iscariot was one of the more important members of the brethren, and his large chambers might include a secret entrance to the tunnels. He had a way of slipping in and out of places unseen, and I needed a place to hide his body before it began to rot.

"What are you doing?" Asira laughed. "You look upset. Are you angry that I'm here? It was your doing, wasn't it?"

I glanced at her wet gown clinging to her curves. If she were sober, she'd be furious, and I needed her to be sober. I needed her mind. The dark and deadly idea that had bloomed only seven days ago returned. Why not enact it? I needed help. "Your being here is not my doing, but I need you to think. What is an herb that counters drugs?"

She snorted and stood, flitting about the room, peering at mirrors and touching the gilded masks. "Depends. If it's a poison, force them to throw up. If it's something that passes through the system, flush them with water and let them sleep it off."

"There's no time to let you sleep it off. Soon, they will return with more."

"It was the wine, wasn't it?"

I nodded. "I told you not to drink it."

"I had to. Besides, I feel good. Better than I ever have. Everything is slightly blurry, though, and you're more handsome than I remember." Asira smiled up at me from under those long eyelashes, her expression coy. "Tell me, that ceremony back there sounded very much like a wedding ceremony. Did we just get married?"

I frowned and stepped back, putting more distance between us. This was not the conversation I wanted to have. At least, not with a drugged Asira. "It's a bonding ceremony. You're here to bring children into the world, nothing more."

"So. I'm married to you now." Asira's nostrils flared, and a hint of her foreboding frown flashed across her face.

I suddenly missed the way her eyes narrowed when I said something she disapproved of. The drug had made her caution fade, a very dangerous situation for both of us.

"Come." I gestured toward the washroom. "Draw a bath and relax."

"A bath? Inside?" Asira stepped into the bedroom, taking in the bed and the open door to the washroom. "Your chambers are quite rich, as I expected."

I turned on the water while Asira stared at me in confusion. Recalling what she said about flushing out the toxins, I returned to the main room and filled a tray with water and food. A note had been left on a bottle, warning that it was the drug and a few drops would suffice. I scowled and almost tossed it into the fireplace, then thought better of it. It might be useful later.

Tucking it into the pocket of my robe, I returned to the washroom and placed the tray on the side of the tub. Group baths were common here, with trays of fruit and wine often served, but Asira wouldn't know that. "Try to eat a bit, and drink lots of water," I told her. "When you're sober, I'll answer all your questions."

I turned to swing the door shut, but Asira's question gave me pause. "Don't you want to join me?"

Pivoting, I met those dark eyes, half-glazed, the edges of confusion shrouding her. I tamped down my frustration and the impulse to kiss her again. With a little shake of my head, I shut the door, wondering if it locked so I could search undisturbed. The last thing I needed was for her to burst out of the room, half naked, while I tried to hide a dead body.

I waited at the door until I heard a splash, then I tore through the room, searching for a secret entrance or a better place to hide the body. Worst-case scenario, I'd have to transport it through the halls, which meant I needed something that wouldn't raise questions or suspicions.

The walls of the room were solid, holding no secret entrances, and I found no trapdoors underneath the carpets. Scrolls and drawings littered a desk, and jewels overflowed on the counters. He was known for wearing thick, heavy rings, and I wished I knew the symbolism of each one. Among the jewels, I found necklaces and earrings, and in the wardrobe, clothing for a female. A cold realization set in as I fingered the silks.

Iscariot knew he'd be mated, and the room had been prepared to share. The clothes and jewels had to be for Asira.

I stroked my jaw, the short stubble rubbing against my fingers. Pretending to be Iscariot wouldn't last long. I had just about seven days to re-discover the clue and come up with a plan to unveil the treachery of the Masters.

Another splash came from the washroom, reminding me of my limited time. Springing into action, I opened a trunk. I'd stuff him in there – later, in the dead of night, I'd sneak down to the tunnels and leave him there. How many would recognize him without his finery and his mask?

After emptying the trunk, I turned to the unpleasant task of stuffing the body into it. Kneeling, I peeked under the bed and yanked my hand back in horror. I stared again to ensure my eyes did not deceive me and slowly, my memories returned.

*This* was the clue I'd discovered.

# II
## ASIRA

I'd never seen such an elaborate washroom. An ivory tub with legs carved in the shape of serpents sat in the center, the edges curling like a budding flower, captured in the moment of unfurling its petals. It was cool to the touch, with tiny glass knobs that made water flow. It was nothing short of sorcery.

I sank into truly hot bathwater, delighting in the way it felt on my skin, and the fact that the tub was so big, I could lie at the bottom and fully immerse myself. This was the luxury I'd always imagined. Soap on my fingertips, I helped myself to sweet grapes, washed down with cold water. The idea entered my mind that the bath was large enough for two, perhaps three, and I giggled at the foolish notion.

Motes of light danced in front of me, and it was difficult for my vision to focus on anything. Worst of all, my mind kept drifting to Drazhan, his low voice in my ear, the way his arms had curved around me while a priest murmured vows over us. It hadn't sunk in until later that it was wedding ceremony.

I should be furious, but the drug in the drink had muted my anger, and a pleasantness buzzed around me. I licked my lips, unable to stop my straying thoughts of undressing Drazhan, moving my lips against his neck, tasting his essence, and...

It was an aphrodisiac, or at least, that was part of the drug. It was mixed with something else to make me feel hazy. A darkness lingered behind my thoughts, and unanswered questions rose and faded because it was too difficult to focus on anything. And why should I?

The water smelled like lilacs as I leaned back, resting my head against the curve of the ivory tub. Warmth surrounded me, and my eyelids fluttered shut. The excitement of the day was catching up with me, and ever since I'd found Drazhan, I hadn't slept well. Now, I was at peace.

THE WATER WAS cold when I woke, and I sat up with a start, my fingers wrinkled, a chill passing over my exposed skin. It was a moment before I recalled that the woozy sensation from being drugged had faded, leaving me with a bitter taste in my mouth and a pang in the pit of my stomach.

Reaching for the tray, I drank some water, groggily climbed out of the tub, and wrapped myself in a fluffy, warm towel. My feet sank into the carpet, and I curled my toes into it, glancing around the washroom for something to wear. My eyes landed on a crimson, rose-patterned robe, right next to a much longer, black robe meant for a man.

My throat went dry at the reminder of what had happened: the flight, the slap, the wine and then... the ceremony. Scrubbing my hand over my face, I let out a low moan. Had I, indeed, just married Drazhan?

My heart kicked at the idea of living together as man and wife. It was certainly not what I wanted, and my knowledge of the tithe had given me no indication that a mating ceremony was to follow. Still, his rooms were large enough for two to live in comfortably, and there was the robe, clearly meant for a woman. I wrapped the velvet around me and towel-dried my hair. With deft fingers I plaited it, ensuring strands still covered the tips of my ears.

I hesitated at the door, unsure what to say when I faced Drazhan. I was quite sure in my drugged state that I'd flirted with him, and my face burned at the idea.

Mated.

Bonded together.

I didn't want to be married, and even though I felt a flair of attraction toward him, I didn't love him. Although, how many times had Grandmother told me love had nothing to do with it?

Marriage was for security, expanding family lines, and easing the burden of work. I'd imagined many things would change for the better when I reached High Terrin, but I never could have imagined this.

Pressing my lips together, I lifted my chin, opened the door, and stepped out.

Soft candlelight lit the room in a halo of gold, highlighting the decor of silver and crimson. Gems sparkled on the chandelier that hung over the bed. I swallowed hard and kept walking. I would not think of the bed or what married couples did on their first night together.

Padding into the main room, I found Drazhan. He looked up when I entered, and I detected a weariness on his face, one that disappeared when he smiled that easy, flirtatious smile. He wore a rich blue robe with gold edging that flowed around his body, and I assumed it must be what the Masters wore day to day. I met his golden eyes and lifted my chin. "We need to talk."

Drazhan gestured to the trays of food that sat on a low table in front of him. "You must be hungry. How do you feel?"

I shrugged. "Not great."

"But no longer drugged?"

"No." I frowned, trying to work out how to start this awkward conversation.

Drazhan lifted the lids off the trays, and the scent of roasted meat made my mouth water. "At least sit and eat, and we can discuss."

I reclined on the couch in front of him and filled my plate. The food of High Terrin was delectable: roasted meat that melted in my mouth, bread still hot from the ovens, fresh fruit and vegetables, and wine, although I only drank water to ease my recovery. The food masked the scent in the air, but underneath that constant floral scent was a hint of dark rot.

As I ate, I considered how to broach the topic of our marriage and what was expected of me in High Terrin, but broad ideas bounced around in my mind until I finally settled on one. "Tell me; how long did you live here before you ended up in the boneyard?"

Drazhan's golden eyes held mine, a seriousness in his steady gaze. "First, Asira, I need to explain. I'm not one of them, not one of the Masters of High Terrin."

"So you've said," I nodded. "I remember."

"Yes, I told you I was sent here on a quest to discover what was wrong with the Masters and destroy them."

I nodded again; these were all things he'd told me before.

Drazhan took a deep breath. "Then you should know this room we're in, it's not mine. During the tithe, I flew up here to take my revenge on the one who cast me down. His name was Iscariot. I took his place, his mask, his room, and...I had no idea it was his turn to take a mate at the tithe, and I didn't know that you'd been chosen."

I sat down the plate of food, my stomach in knots.

Drazhan leaned forward and dropped his voice. "I wanted to bring you here with me, but I needed to ensure it was safe first, and I couldn't remember exactly what had happened to me."

"But you do now?" I confirmed.

He nodded, and his gaze shifted away, as though he had something to hide. Another wave of disquiet came over me, and I picked up a goblet of water, just to give myself something else to focus on.

I studied the room as I waited, giving him a chance to tell me more. The wardrobe was open, displaying rows of beautiful clothes. Half of them were robes, the other half of them dresses, all meant for a woman. *Me?*

If not for Drazhan, I would have been wed to Iscariot, and I wondered what kind of bridegroom he would have made. Then there was the drug, and if the Masters were using drugs, something was *very* wrong. I turned my attention back to Drazhan, desperate to make sense of what was happening in High Terrin.

Drazhan finally spoke, his voice haunted. "When I was here before, investigating the Masters, I discovered their true identity, what they look like behind their masks."

"I thought they looked like you," I said.

"So did I, but they don't. There's a reason they hide behind their masks."

My brows furrowed. "Because they are hideous?"

"Monstrous, in fact. I didn't remember until I confronted Iscariot, and it all came whirling back. When I met you, I had the sense you could help me, and we could work together to unravel the secrets of the Masters."

I frowned. "Why me?"

"Because you're the Stardust Collector, and you have fae blood."

My back went stiff, and my jaw worked. "How do you know?" I whispered.

"I've seen your pointed ears, and you have healing power in your fingertips. I'm certain it was you who woke me in the boneyard, who brought me back to life."

My lips thinned. "I can't raise the dead."

"No, but I am immortal, and when wounded, I sleep for a long time unless awoken. My body wasn't fully knitted back together, but all the same, I felt you."

Me. I blinked and leaned back, refusing to look at him. "Yes, I am a healer, but how does that help you up here?"

"Because you're also fae, an old enemy of the Masters. It was said that during the war, the fae learned the secrets of the Masters and how to destroy them, which is partially why the Masters took to the skies: to escape."

My pulse quickened. This was the story I wanted to know, the one I'd hoped my grandmother would share with me. I had wanted to come to High Terrin to learn the truth, and here Drazhan was, sharing it with me. I held up a hand, stopping him. "Just because I have fae blood doesn't mean I know anything about the war or the secrets shared in that day. Besides, you could ask anyone in Terrin; they all believe iron is what harms the Masters, which is why they never set foot on the ground."

Drazhan frowned. "No, that's just a legend. The Masters use iron, and there's no correlation between iron and the ground. There's another reason they don't set foot on Terrin, but I haven't found it yet. You're smart, Asira, and quick. I think you could help me figure this out, especially if I tell you everything I know."

I tilted my head, eyeing him. "Why would I want to help you destroy the Masters? They protect Terrin from monsters and brought me here to dwell with them in luxury."

"You're not here to dwell here in luxury..." Drazhan trailed off, his eyes clouded. "You're here to work."

I pinched the bridge of my nose. "Work? To do what I did in Terrin up here?"

"No. The truth is, the Masters are dying. They cannot reproduce, but the mortals are fruitful and multiply. The Masters have concluded it is something in their blood. Hence, during the annual tithe, five young men are taken for their blood, and five young women are taken to become the new mothers."

I blanched. "Mothers? Then why was I bonded to you during the ceremony?"

"Because it is our turn to mate and produce children. If it is not done within three months, they will take you."

# 12

## DRAZHAN

Asira stared at me, eyes wide as the knowledge sank in. "This is why we never see those who are chosen again, isn't it? At least, if what you say is true."

I leaned forward, holding her gaze. "It is true, and no one asks because they believe the Masters are protectors."

Asira resumed eating, her expression impossible to read. "What is your plan, then? I'm here, but without knowledge of the secrets of the fae. How do you propose we find said secrets without you ending up in the boneyard again?"

I took a sip of wine, letting the bold flavors bloom on my tongue. One benefit to living in High Terrin was that the Masters were provided with the best of everything. Still, I'd exchange this luxury any day to force them to atone for their crimes. "My theory is that it has something to do with stardust."

Asira gave me a deadpan look. "Stardust does have magical properties, but it's used for healing."

I paused, torn between telling her exactly what had happened with Iscariot and fearing how she'd react when she learned I was storing a dead body in the room. A body I might not get to move until nightfall, if I were lucky. "Meant to heal, yes," I confirmed, unable to get the picture of Iscariot's body out of my mind. "But what if...it harms them?"

Asira stood up and stared pacing, the crimson robe swirling around her ankles. I leaned back, enjoying her take-charge attitude. It was good to brainstorm, to discuss options with her instead of sitting here alone. Was I enjoying the companionship too much? After all, what the Masters did was dark and serious. They should be called to judgment as soon as possible.

At last, Asira pointed at me. "We need proof. It's no use dreaming up theories without proof."

I hated to admit that she was right; what if Iscariot was an isolated case? "True, and I need to gather more stardust."

"You have stardust? Here?"

"I took some from your cottage when I left and stored it in the tunnels here. I figured it would be handy if—"

"Something happened to you again," she finished.

I nodded, watching her brow furrow as thoughts raced through her mind.

"After you get stardust, then what?" Asira asked.

"I'm still thinking through that part."

Asira tapped her chin and glanced at the door. "What do the Masters want from us, now that we are...married? Is there a routine they expect us to follow?"

I grimaced. "I believe so. We have a quiet week, and then the official celebration. It is a banquet with dining, drinking, and dancing."

"Will everyone be there? Including the chosen?"

"Yes," I responded, staring at the ground. Last year, what had I seen? Glazed eyes, painted on smiles, and a hint of something darker. I should have fought harder to save them.

Asira wrinkled her nose. "So, all this time, I thought being chosen was a great honor. Instead, they drug them and force them to mate." She broke off, shivering. "That alone is vile and disgusting enough to judge them."

"Now you understand."

Asira pinned me with her dark eyes. "But who are we to condemn the Masters? They are above us, our protectors..."

"It's not an easy task. I was close, so close, before. But then they discovered who I am. I sense we are at the very edge of unlocking the truth, and perhaps you will be the key to their downfall and freeing Terrin."

"Freedom has different meanings. Without the Masters, the monsters might ravish the land."

"True, but what if there are no monsters at all, at least, not anymore?"

Asira snorted. "As though all the legends were lies?"

I had no response, for she was correct about many things. Instead, I held out my hand to her. "Come, sit with me. We don't have to discuss this anymore."

She wrapped her arms around herself, shrinking in as though she had no wish to be near me. "But we do. It's the sole reason I'm here."

Standing, I approached her, sliding my hands up her arms. She shivered at the contact but did not move away. The fragrance of her skin and hair was intoxicating, but with her, I had to move slowly and let her accept my touch.

Gently, I slide a finger under her silk robe, exposing her neck and collarbone. Asira drew a shuddering breath as her lips parted and her eyelids fluttered shut.

Ever so slowly, I dropped my head and pressed my lips against her neck. A tiny gasp left her lips, encouraging me.

Asira made me want things I never dreamed I could have, and the idea of a future with her was intoxicating. She smelled of flowers with a hint of stardust, and the herbs from the forest that never completely left her skin.

My heart thundered in my chest as I trailed kisses down her neck and along her collarbone, wanting to go fast but knowing she needed me to go slow.

When at last I pressed my lips to hers, a low sound ripped from her throat, and this time, she reciprocated with hot, thirsty kisses that left us both panting.

Sinking to my knees in front of her, I tilted my head up while she rested a shaking hand on my shoulder. "I quite like you, Asira of Terrin," I admitted. "But I honor and respect you, so I will not share your bed unless you invite me."

She squeezed my shoulder, pupils dilated as she whispered, "Not yet."

*Yet.*

I counted that as a victory.

Later that night, once Asira had gone to sleep, I wavered in indecision at the door. I needed to bring weapons and stardust up from the tunnels, but should any of the Masters burst into the room, she'd be unprotected.

I'd seen what they did to the mothers, keeping them drugged at all times so that they would be amicable and willing. After a time, they were taken to the sanctum—an inner tower—where the Masters drank their blood and experimented on them in the hopes of producing more Masters.

All to no avail.

The Masters were growing old. In a hundred years, give or take, their line would die out, which made them desperate.

It was too early for them to take Asira, and too dangerous for me to attempt to move Iscariot's body. However, we needed protection, so I opened the door and left.

The halls were silent as I slipped down them, attempting to carry myself like Iscariot would, shoulders high, chin lifted, barreling toward a destination with no remorse.

Occasionally, sounds drifted from behind closed doors: muted growls, higher pitched laughs, and ever so often, a whimper or cry. Those mournful sounds only stiffened my resolve.

The Masters enjoyed sadistic pleasures, especially after a celebration. They often went too far with their obsession with blood.

I did what I could by making some of the Masters disappear, leaving their masks and hair in odd places, caught on tree branches near the edge of the floating kingdom or stuffed under the tunnels where the beast dwelled.

Then, the rumors started.

Someone within the circle wished harm upon some of the Masters and was secretly killing them.

It was Iscariot who became the leader of the investigation, and he who'd eventually found me, punished me, and cast me down.

What had he told the others?

Most likely, he bragged about his conquest while the kingdom enjoyed peace for six months.

Six months.

Dread coursed through me at what had happened while I was gone. Lost in my musing, I startled when clawed fingers gripped my arm, holding so tight, they cut through the voluminous fabric of my robe.

"Iscariot," a low voice hissed.

I knew that voice, that tone, and those fingers.

Curses.

I'd forgotten he roamed the halls at night, ensuring everyone was in their place. With a sinking sensation, I turned, steeling myself against the bad breath of Alder.

I'd always hated Alder and his superiority over the Masters. While he wasn't the leader, he was in charge of the inner circle and the tower where the mortals were kept. He enjoyed his duties of bloodletting far too much and now stood over me, judging.

"Release me," I snapped hoarsely, knowing if I pulled away, Alder's claws would draw blood. Once he drew blood, he'd taste it and know I wasn't one of them.

The claw tightened. "Aren't you supposed to be in bed with your new conquest?"

"It's not much of a conquest when we invite them here and drug them."

"I thought you'd be more eager for your turn between the legs of one of them."

Blood roared in my ears, and I held myself back from punching him across his masked mouth. Why had I left Asira alone in the room, unguarded?

"She's sleeping."

"Huh." The claw retreated but Alder leaned closer. "I picked her especially for you, Iscariot. Don't make me regret the choice."

Alder moved past, intentionally bumping my shoulder and sniffing the air.

I hurried away. Alder was keen and would know if something was wrong. He never trusted me and always turned up when least expected. I wasn't sure if Iscariot and Alder were friends; from the brief exchange, I assumed there was some level of comradeship, but it did not bypass threats. Quickening my pace, I hurried to the tunnels, hoping I was right about stardust.

# 13
## ASIRA

I had a purpose.

That thought kept me wide awake long after Drazhan said goodnight and left me to sleep, alone, in that enormous bed. Against my sensibilities, I kept reliving the moment when he parted my robe and kissed my neck and shoulders. The act was so intimate, so sensual, I'd given in to his caress without reservation. My skin heated at the reminder of the taste of his mouth, coaxing me out of my shell, making me burn for him.

He was an immortal Master, and I was the Stardust Collector. At least, I had been when I lived down below. Now?

Our paths had drawn us together, and I could almost see my grandmother wagging her finger at me, telling me it was fate, and I should play my part as expected. Did my part include falling for Drazhan?

He was unexpected, and how he treated me with thoughtfulness and consideration left me unsure how to react. I'd assumed marriage was simply a transaction, a give and take, the sharing of strengths and weaknesses all geared toward survival. Drazhan showed me the benefits of companionship and...I dared to think it...how much enjoyment could be gained from spending time together.

Rustling came from the main room, and I sat up in bed. A quiet step sounded, and then the door shut with a muffled click. I pressed my lips together, my skin hot at the idea of him. He'd told me he'd gone in search of weapons and stardust during an hour when many remained behind closed doors. What did the Masters do with their time? I longed to know and to see more of the palace and the grounds.

Restless, I climbed out of bed, wishing I could open a window and let in fresh, cool air. The room was warm enough, yet the scent was stale, the foul odor growing stronger. How was I supposed to unravel the secrets of High Terrin in a week?

I ran my fingers through my hair, my hands anxious to be doing something. I'd never imagined being bored in the floating kingdom, but without my healing supplies, I had nothing to do.

I tried not to think of the other young women who'd been chosen and what they might be enduring. Determination gave me steely courage as I recalled the way the Master slapped Sari, as if her attachment to earthen things was not allowed.

My thoughts kept straying to the things I'd be doing if I were home in my cozy cottage. Probably making notes of how much stardust I had left. Grandmother had a habit of keeping a written account of everything, including treatments, healing remedies, and payments received.

I paused.

What if the Masters kept a similar account of the chosen ones? Wouldn't they have a room where those records were stored? If so, Drazhan might be able to share some knowledge regarding it, and at last, I'd find out more, perhaps even discover the secrets the fae knew.

Climbing back into bed, I resolved to wait until Drazhan returned.

I leaned back against the pillows, and the next thing I knew, I awoke to beams of sunlight dancing on my face.

Light shone in from a circular window, the only one in the room, as though light was not something the Masters preferred. Pulling on my robe, I strode toward the wardrobe to pick out something to wear.

"There she is," Drazhan said.

I peeked over my shoulder as I opened the wardrobe. Drazhan appeared, effortlessly handsome as usual, dressed in emerald edged with golden swirls. A gilded mask was by his side, as if he expected the door to burst open any moment.

Standing, he leaned against the doorway, watching me.

I bit back my smile and returned my focus to the clothes. "I have an idea," I announced.

"Is that so?"

"We are allowed to leave this room, aren't we?"

Drazhan shrugged. "Within reason."

"I assume there is a room of records here? A place where written accounts are stored?"

He nodded. "There is, but for the most part, it is off-limits."

I picked out a dress and faced Drazhan, gesturing to his mask. "You aren't just Drazhan anymore, though; I'm sure you'll think of a way for us to access it."

He grinned. "Asira, I do believe you're brilliant."

I flushed and headed toward the washroom to dress.

THE WEEK FELL into somewhat of a routine, the night of the banquet drawing ever closer while Drazhan and I snuck about the palace, searching for clues.

My favorite place was the archives. Drazhan's lofty status as one of the Masters granted him access, or rather, it was Iscariot's mask that was the key. He was allowed to come and go as often as he pleased, and he snuck me in three days in a row.

The archives were not very organized, with scrolls, stacks of paper, and unbound books overflowing everywhere. Some of the Masters worked there, illuminating texts, copying down older records, and working by large windows that let in plenty of light.

I did my best to avoid them, and even at times sent Drazhan away under the guise that it was easier to stay hidden without him there. I knew he feared for me, even though I wore a vial of stardust around my neck, as promised. I had the sense that Drazhan knew more than he'd shared with me, but I wanted to unravel the truth for myself.

On the third day, I discovered a scroll with details about the war and references to the fae. There was one small problem: only half of it was written in a language I understood. The other was in some ancient text. I bit back my anticipation, hoping that Drazhan would be able to read it. I was sure the answers lay there, hidden in the text.

# 14
# DRAZHAN

Asira paced as I read the words of the scroll out loud to her, translating slowly to ensure I inferred the correct meaning. I waited patiently while she listened, wrinkling her nose as I attempted to discern a deeper meaning.

"There's nothing here," I said at last, re-reading the last paragraph. "The only mention of the fae and the war is that they laid their hands upon the Masters and damned them. No mention of a secret."

Asia's shoulders slumped. "I was sure I had something, but you're so sure that they dislike stardust. Why?"

I shifted, glancing at the corner of the room where the chest had been. A few nights ago, I'd been able to sneak Iscariot's body out of the room and into the tunnels. Beyond that, it was too dangerous to move him, too many comings and goings. I still worried that someone would discover him, and I certainly didn't want to show Asira his body as proof. Still, she was right: we needed proof.

"Tonight is the banquet; perhaps an opportunity to test my theory will arise there. I believe the Masters have a bad reaction to the stardust against their skin. But that's the problem: they wear masks, long robes, and gloves. One never sees their true appearance."

"So you hope to catch them unaware, when their guard is down during a night of inhibitions."

I smiled at her. She ducked her head and shifted away, but I knew she was warming to me.

Sometimes, she strayed too near, lingering with a hand on my shoulder, waiting for one of my impulsive kisses. She enjoyed those, even though she pretended not to.

After a beat, her eyes danced back to mine, holding my gaze as something there softened. I half rose when a tap came at the door.

Asira didn't hesitate. She fled into the adjoining chamber while I marched toward the door, then doubled back and snatched up the wig and mask. After hastily checking my appearance in the looking glass, I cracked open the door.

A golden mask glimmered back at me, a star-shaped symbol on the left cheek.

"Iscariot," he whispered.

"Jabel," I grunted.

He punched my arm. "Having fun yet? Where is she?"

"Asleep," I shrugged, my fingers closing into a fist.

"Oh, well, when you get tired of your new possession, it's happening tonight, after the banquet."

I hadn't the faintest idea what might be happening. "Come and remind me, lest I get carried away."

Jabel snorted. "You lucky bastard. Are the humans really as...you know..."

I eased the door shut. "Later, Jabel."

Leaning against the closed door, I glanced at the scroll again. Shame it hadn't revealed any secrets. Apparently, whatever the fae knew about the Masters, they had taken with them into another realm. It was a foolish idea to involve Asira in this madness. Tonight, I would take the stardust and ruin them.

Inside the wardrobe, I discovered clothes for the ceremony: a suit of black and gold for myself and a dress of silver and gold for Asira. I laid them on the foot of the bed and slipped into the washroom to bathe and prepare.

When I stepped back out, fully dressed, Asira was also dressed and standing in front of one of the full-length looking glasses.

I paused in the doorway, for Asira had transformed from the simple Stardust Collector, with a stain on her gown, to someone else, someone wondrous.

The gown gathered around her throat, leaving her back bare, while a ruffled train swept the ground, showing off her legs in the front. The thin material molded to her body, leaving nothing to the imagination. I fought to rein in my jealousy, aware I wanted nothing more than to hide her in the room.

She peeked over her shoulder then turned around, loose curls gracing her shoulders. I crossed the room to her in three long strides, cupping her face and brushing my lips over hers.

She stilled.

I held the kiss, waiting until she melted against me, her lips parting and hands coming up to grip my arms. I deepened the kiss, rewarded with a soft moan as she tilted her head back, pressing her body against mine. It was tempting to push her back against the bed and make sweet love to her.

When I pulled back, her eyes were depthless pools of desire, and she cleared her throat, teeth dragging at her bottom lip, enticing me to kiss her again. That cold defiance returned, but she didn't pull away. Fingertips touched my hand, not quite stroking but not pulling my hand away either.

"We've delayed long enough, and I can't help but think about the other Chosen. We can't stand by and let them endure another week here. We need to take action and get proof."

Nodding, I caught her hand and kissed it. "Tonight."

# 15
## ASIRA

I craned my neck, taking in the sights as I walked down the hall on Drazhan's arm. Chandeliers hung from the peaked ceiling, glittering crystals catching the ebb and flow of light. Columns of gold dotted the hall, while paintings and glass frescos covered the walls. My eyes rounded, and moisture filled my mouth as I stared at the banquet.

Golden tables filled the space, Masters weaving between them, taking their seats. To one side, musicians warmed up their instruments. In front of the banquet tables was an open space, I guessed for dancing. Nothing as elaborate as this display had taken place in Terrin. There was even a bonfire in the center, smoke escaping through a hole in the ceiling. Three boars roasted over the fire, slowly turned by masked cooks.

My mouth watered. All week long, I'd had the luxury of eating meat, and I was starting to get used to it.

"Only eat or drink what I give you," Drazhan whispered.

I gave him a stiff nod, my fingers tightening on his arm.

Stringed instruments hummed as we took our seats, and I noticed other females, humans I assumed, for they wore similar clothing to myself, which left plenty of skin exposed. The females wore masks—as did I—but they only covered our eyes. I glanced around the hall again. Were there no female Masters?

As I leaned toward Drazhan to ask, a pungent odor stung my nose. A hunched figure holding a staff lumbered up to us and placed a hand encased in a hard, gold glove on Drazhan's shoulder. I stared at the glove, taking in the claws on its tips. I couldn't say why, but a vision of horror filled my mind and my stomach twisted.

"Iscariot, I see you have arrived," the Master said.

Drazhan kept his face forward, as though the hand clenching his shoulder did not bother him. "Alder. Is there something you want from me?"

"To ensure you will be in your place tonight," Alder hissed. "I know how easily you get distracted."

Drazhan grunted in response, and the masked face turned to me.

I stared, dread growing in my heart. For the first time, I found the golden masks rather sinister. It completely covered Alder's face; even his eyes were hidden behind the gaping black slits of his mask.

I shifted in my seat, wondering if I'd covered my ears enough. What if the Masters discovered the truth about my bloodline?

"Well, you are quite lovely, aren't you?" Alder said. "Welcome to High Terrin."

A wave of nauseousness almost overpowered me, but I was supposed to be drugged and giddy with happiness. Forcing my lips into a smile, I nodded. "Thank you."

Alder paused for a long moment before moving on, taking the overpowering stench with him.

I faced forward, heart pounding as I fisted my hands in my lap. A malevolent aura came from him, and it frightened me. It wasn't until Drazhan dropped a hand into my lap that my trembling faded.

As the seats across from us filled, I dropped my voice to a whisper. "Who was that?"

Drazhan took a grape from the table, rolling it between his fingers before slipping it under his mask and into his mouth. The movement was effortless and revealed no hint of what might lie underneath. Was that how all the Masters ate?

"Alder is the leader of the brethren, the elite Masters. He takes care of those who have...disappointed the kingdom."

"Why does he smell like that?"

"I've never caught him in the act, but my guess is that he drinks blood."

I choked on my own spit, drawing attention as I coughed. Drazhan passed me a glass of water and I took a sip, my mind racing. The Masters drank *blood*?

What other truths had Drazhan hidden from me? A bloom of red caught my eye, and I glanced at his shoulder. "You're bleeding," I rasped.

Drazhan jerked, glanced at his shoulder and cursed. "He'll test my blood and find the truth. We have little time."

A chime rang out, and silence fell over the hall. One of the Masters, dressed in a white robe, rose and spoke. He welcomed the Chosen and congratulated the Masters on another successful year, then asked that we raise a toast to the future of High Terrin.

When he finished, applause filled the hall. More masked Masters brought in food, setting a heaping plate in front of everyone, then adding extra trays to the tables.

Conversation erupted across the room, filling it with the joyous sound of celebration. The musicians struck up their instruments, and my fingers curled around a goblet of water. My throat was tight as questions whirled through my mind. Drazhan had said that the Masters were hideous, that they had to hide their true appearance. What could they possibly look like?

I studied the other women, watching their mannerisms. Their masks hid their eyes but left their nose and mouth exposed. They appeared happy, giddy, and likely drugged.

I furrowed my brow. What was so terrible that they couldn't be in their natural state? Were the Masters that hideous?

Drazhan rose and touched my shoulder. "Let's dance," he said as he drew me to the dance floor.

# 16
## DRAZHAN

It was only a matter of time before Alder discovered I was an imposter. The vial of star-dust corded around my neck wouldn't be enough, nor would the ones I'd stuffed in my pocket.

I'd given some to Asira, and her curls hid the leather cord that held the vials. The palace wasn't safe for Asira, and if I disappeared, the Masters would become suspicious. What if they found Iscariot's body in the tunnels?

I had no doubt that even if Asira and I fled to Terrin, the Masters would chase us down on their golden chariots, determined to take back what they believed was theirs and get their revenge on me.

My arms tightened around Asira's waist. Shame I couldn't fully enjoy how wonderful she felt in my arms, all soft curves and silky hair. I wanted to bury my face in her hair and forget about this madness.

At first, she was stiff, unwilling to move, leaving me wondering if she danced at all. Asira had been tight-lipped about her life, but as the Stardust Collector, she was well-known to the people of Terrin. Now, I wondered at her need to escape and whether her position in Terrin had been what she wanted. She did her work well, but just because one was good at what one's job did not make it the desire of their heart.

Something within had made her unhappy enough to wish herself here. I stared at her upturned face as she let me guide her through the steps. The mask hid her eyes, and her lips were set in an impassive frown, making it difficult to guess what she was thinking.

We weren't the only ones who whirled around the dance floor. When a hand landed on my shoulder, I resisted the urge to flinch it off as someone leaned closer, a symbol I did not recognize glowing on their mask. "A chance to dance with your new beloved?"

The idea of anyone other than myself laying hands on Asira made a protective jealousy rise in my chest. "Not a chance," I growled.

"Not a chance, eh? So, your words earlier were flippant. You promised to share, but it was all a ruse to get your way. I won't forget this, Iscariot."

I stiffened. The problem with pretending to be Iscariot was that I had no idea what had happened during the last six months. Before I was cast down, I was familiar with his inner circle. Perhaps not their conversations, but I could deduce what was happening and the dynamics of power. Now, I could not detect where the balance of power laid.

Asira spun in my arms and then whirled away from me. The sea of gilded masks converged, creating a barrier between us. I lost sight of her dark hair, and my hand went to my pocket, gripping the vial of stardust as they surrounded me.

"Come, Iscariot," Jabel laughed. "It's time."

Time for some haunted ceremony I had no idea about. I glanced back, searching for Asira, aware that asking what would happen to her would give me away. Iscariot cared for naught but himself, and I had to play the game a while longer, at least until Adler discovered my secret.

"Don't worry," another said. "You'll have plenty of time with your new playmate. She'll be in your chambers, waiting for you."

# 17
## ASIRA

Dancing calmed my nerves, giving me something to focus on other than the unsettling glamour of the Masters. Drazhan's arm around me was firm, a reminder I had someone on my side. What would have happened if I hadn't met him in the boneyard and saved him? I'd be doomed right now, one of the forgotten humans who went up to the starry kingdom for the pleasure of the Masters.

The other women appeared happy, but when I spun by one, the glazed look on her face made my heart hurt. She wasn't truly there. Her soul was lost, bound in darkness, begging to be freed.

My throat tightened, and I turned away. Something was very wrong.

Drazhan's grip on me relaxed as one hand spanned my hip, spinning me away from him. I twirled, letting go of his hand as my hair swung down my back. I glimpsed the musicians, wearing golden masks and playing with enthusiasm.

Tapestries glimmered, diamonds winked, glasses clicked, and the murmur of conversation swept around me, making my skin prickle. Turning around, I reached for Drazhan, but he was gone, lost in a sea of masks. My heart kicked, but I took a deep breath. The golden hair all looked the same, and I hadn't memorized the mark on his mask.

Iscariot's mask.

I felt a presence at my back, and then hands slithered around my waist. A faint odor surrounded me, and then a voice that certainly wasn't Drazhan's coasted across my ear. "He didn't drug you, did he? Very curious and quite unlike Iscariot."

"I don't know what you're talking about," I retorted. Try as I might, I couldn't force myself to be silly and giggly. I wasn't sure who stood behind me, but a warning in my soul told me to run.

Another Master hooked their arm around mine. "I'm sure Iscariot won't mind if we have some fun with you. He did promise to share."

I struggled to get free, suddenly reminded of when the wayward knight had attacked me. My arm was yanked behind my back, the movement jarring and painful. I winced and squirmed. "Let go of me," I hissed, trying not to rouse attention.

Lips nibbled up my arm to my neck, and then teeth sank into my skin, not painful, but shocking and uncomfortable. I let out a yelp and brought my knee up fast.

The Master stepped back and lifted a hand. The slap of his glove against my skin sent my head rocking back. A dull roar rushed through my mind, and a bubble of darkness rose in my chest.

Behind me came laughter, and my fury twisted like a whirlwind. My fingers flew to my neck, practically ripping my dress as I yanked the vial of stardust off the chain.

Snarling, I uncorked the bottle and threw the contents at the Master who'd bitten me.

Stardust glittered in the air, beautiful and dazzling, and I watched it fall across the Master's masked face. Would it do anything, or was Drazhan wrong?

An inhuman shriek drowned out the sound of music, and the Master stumbled back, holding his face. His mask tumbled to the ground and my jaw dropped.

Smoke curled from his fingers where his gloves had been burned away. The guttural scream came again, a bellow of deep, intense pain. The Master dropped his hands, revealing bulbous red eyes and dark leathery skin melting away under stardust, as though he'd been burned.

I gasped, bile rising in my throat as the other Master leaped at me.

Spinning, I tossed more stardust at him, getting the same reaction: a shriek of pain, a tossed mask, and then the reveal of curved, pointed ears, leathery skin, red eyes, a sunken nose, and curved fangs.

I didn't wait to see more; spinning on my heel, I ran.

Drazhan had been right about the stardust.

My fairytale of a glorious kingdom in the clouds had turned into a nightmare. I'd walked straight into the pit of hell, and all those dark and deadly beasts surrounded me.

Beings with red eyes and leathery skin. Foul beasts. Monsters. Demons.

Where was Drazhan? I needed him now!

Shaking, I fled down the hallway, desperately trying to catch my breath. My chest was tight, and my stomach roiled. Any moment, I expected leering masks to bear down on me, but only darkness glared back when I peered over my shoulder.

At last, I burst out of the palace, and crisp fall air slapped me across the face. I sank to my knees, gasping, hand pressed to my heart as I sucked in deep breaths of air. No, I couldn't stop; they were too close. I had to hide, then find a way to escape from the floating islands.

Staggering upright, I continued down a path. The stars glimmered like jewels in the obsidian blackness of the night sky, and a slice of moonlight gave me just enough light to see in front of me. It was much brighter up here versus down in my tiny cottage, where trees partially covered the sky.

Shapes rose in the gloom, some kind of mounds. It was only when I neared that I realized they were statues, gleaming white carvings of nymphs and satyrs, dryads and centaurs. None of them were human, but some variation of an immortal and a creature: curved horns, goat hooves, fish tails, and wings.

One creature wasn't carved of marble, black as night, almost impossible to see until I was upon it. It had the wings of a gigantic bird but a long neck, heavily scaled, and the snout of a lizard.

A prickling sensation went up my spine.

The creature swirled its head, and golden eyes startled me. Stunned, I stepped back, and the ground swallowed me whole.

# 18
## DRAZHAN

The overpowering scent of blood was all I could smell as we moved into the inner sanctum. It was difficult to pretend to be Iscariot, for he'd been here many times, and this was my first. My gloved hands tightened as I studied the chamber, and my pulse pounded as my worst suspicions were confirmed.

The young men who had been chosen for the tithe lay in the room, shackled to their beds, used for bloodletting and nothing more. Even a few of the barren women had ended up in this haunted place, bodies preserved, their blood feeding the Masters. I suspected Alder also feasted on their flesh after they died of weakness.

My fingers went to the vials of stardust. In one action, one moment, I could destroy them all, yet I hesitated. I'd left Asira exposed, surrounded by Masters. If I acted, would that put her in harm's way? Stardust would only go so far.

An elbow jabbed me in the ribs. It would be typical to respond with violence; instead, I stepped away, scowling behind my mask.

A goblet sat on a column in the middle of the room. I was familiar with this kind of dark initiation. I walked to it as the chanting began. Iscariot was a leader of the circle, but he had a level of disrespect that often got him into trouble. Tonight, I hoped it would play in my favor.

While they chanted, I uncorked a vial of stardust and poured it into the goblet. A shared drink was a signature of the gathered brethren, and I was certain, at some point, they'd share the goblet. Unfortunately, instead of wine, it was filled with thick, red blood. The stardust glittered on it. Would they notice? Would it be enough?

A step came, heavy and slow, as Alder entered the chamber. Stepping back from the goblet, I returned to my place beside Jabel as the chanting died away.

Alder lifted his hands and placed them on either side of his mask. "My brethren, we have gathered once again to celebrate the future of our reign here in High Terrin. Decades ago, we warred with the fae and sought sanctuary here, establishing a kingdom above the world, beyond their reach. Our numbers diminished, we were left with a choice: find a way to reproduce or endure our curse and fade. For years, we have battled the blight, aware that our numbers could not increase unless we joined with the humans. Now, the future is clear. Two will become mothers within the year, which is why we celebrate. The winds of fate have changed, and this will be the start of a new empire. Tonight, we drink to the coming change."

His hands tightened around his mask and lifted.

An audible gasp filled the chamber, and I stepped back, dread filling my heart.

Alder had loose, leathery skin hanging off his brittle bones. Red eyes gleamed in his grinning skull. Instead of a nose, there were two holes in his skeletal face, and curved fangs cut into his dry, chapped lips.

He was a hideous demon.

"Tonight, we stand before each other as unmasked brethren. Let us share a drink and show our true faces. Soon, a day will come where we'll no longer need to hide, for the world will revere and worship us as their saviors."

One by one, the Masters removed their masks, revealing their demonic appearance. The younger ones had leathery skin stretched over their bones. They all had fangs and variations of pointed ears, claws, tails, and round orbs for eyes.

It was as I feared.

When I'd thrown stardust at Iscariot, he'd been wearing a glamor. It was the stardust that revealed his true form and burned his skin. I was unsure if all the Masters were demons, or if it were just Iscariot, but tonight's revelation gave me the dreaded proof I'd been seeking.

Readying myself for what was to come, I removed my mask, the golden hair floating to the ground. Luminous eyes turned to me, and a guttural gasp floated through the room.

Jabel spoke first. "What have you done with Iscariot?"

Making a fist, I backed away. "Come any closer, and you'll find out."

"You're supposed to be dead," someone else echoed.

"Iscariot bragged about killing you six months ago."

"How is this possible?"

Alder's dry tone cut through the chatter. "Rest assured my brethren. Drazhan, the face changer, shall get what he deserves. I called you here for a reason, and since he is not one of us, he won't know how to escape."

I took another step back, eyes narrowed. How difficult could it be to escape? I'd spent the past year studying the habits of the Masters, learning their weaknesses. Stardust was the missing weapon, and now that I had it, it was time for judgment day.

I opened my fist and hurled the stardust at Adler.

# 19
## ASIRA

Talons curled around my waist, ripping at the flimsy material of my dress. A blast of cold air seared my skin, and I bit back a scream as I was lifted out of the hole and up into the midnight sky.

My heart dipped as a weightlessness came over me, worse than it had been on the chariot ride. I had a strong impulse to squirm until it dropped me, but reason won over. Wherever this creature was taking me could not be worse than a castle full of hellish demons.

At last, the winged creature dropped me, and I landed with a thump on soft earth. My teeth were chattering, and I lay still, too afraid to move. My side throbbed from where talons had dug into my flesh, and when I put my hand there, warm blood oozed out.

I was too numb to fully feel the pain, but once I warmed up, I would. One vial of stardust still hung around my throat. I needed it to both heal and defend myself, but first, I needed to find a warm place to hide.

Cold wind blew around me as the creature gave an ear-shrieking cry and lifted, wings flapping as it flew away.

Alone, I listened.

Occasionally, a chill breeze blew, and in the distance was the sound of swiftly flowing water. I willed myself to sit up, the starlight giving me light.

In the distance, I spied the golden towers of the Masters' castle, but the depth of darkness separating me from it led me to believe I was no longer on the main floating island. There were three islands, all linked together by a thin strip of land, with the largest one in the middle and two smaller ones beside it.

I guessed the winged beast had brought me to one of the smaller islands to feast, but no signs of a nest revealed itself. Hugging my bare shoulders, I turned my back on the golden castle and faced the darkness. As my eyes adjusted, I saw a hump. Was that a home in the hillside?

I licked my dry lips and limped toward it. If devils lived there, I was in no shape to fight, but perhaps I could hide. Thoughts of Drazhan flickered to the forefront, and I glanced back, wondering what might be happening to him.

One week ago, my spirits had soared when I was chosen, and I had believed Drazhan had granted my wish. Now? How far I'd fallen from the heights of that moment and the euphoria of dwelling within the starry kingdom.

Why hadn't I been happy with my simple life? My desire for more than the life my grandmother lived had introduced me to horror. What I would give to be back on the ground in my cottage, impatiently waiting for the next wounded soul to arrive at my door.

As soon as I found shelter, I'd make a plan to escape. I could no longer stay in Terrin, for fear the Masters would come for redemption. No, I had to pack up my belongings and follow the road elsewhere.

My heart sank, for the idea of starting over was daunting. Would I find another village in need of a Stardust Collector or healer?

The land sloped down then rose again, bringing me to the doorstep of the house in the hill. My fingertips grazed the door, finding it ajar. Whoever lived here had left in a hurry and forgotten to shut the door. Perhaps that meant they were still gone.

Gripping my last vial of stardust tight, I pushed open the door and prepared to hurl it into the face of a demon.

Silver light shone in, displaying an empty, circular room. It was a simple home: a floor made of reeds, a pallet on the floor, and a circle of ash where they probably kept a fire. Directly above shone a beam of moonlight, filling the space with light. I ached to light a fire, but there was no wood, and it would only be a signal, pointing to my hiding spot.

I studied the room again, eyes landing on a chest I'd overlooked. With trembling fingers, I pushed it open, finding thick blankets and robes inside. It only confirmed my suspicions. One of the demons dwelled here. Why? What would entice one to dwell so far away from everyone else?

Quickly, I stripped off my dress and buried it in the bottom of the chest. Shivering, I set about examining my wounds. Slices of the skin around my waist had been ripped away, and I gingerly applied stardust, aware I needed to save some to defend myself. If I were at home, I'd make a tincture to drink as well, but here, I had to grit my teeth and bear the pain.

Wrapping myself in blankets to keep out the chill, I made a nest on the pallet and huddled into it, stardust in hand, watching the door.

# 20

## DRAZHAN

A comet of stardust streaked in an arc, bits of it touching every Master assembled. They hissed as they stepped back, red eyes glowing as they surrounded me. I backed away, my eyes scanning the room for weapons. I'd already wasted a vial of stardust on the cup of blood, and I only had one more with me.

"Kill him," Alder ordered, leering with pleasure at my hesitation.

I leaped back, searching for the exit as the demons attacked. A flurry of claws and fangs filled my vision. Uncorking the last vial of stardust, I hurled it at them, my ears ringing as horrific shrieks went up.

The skin of the demons burned, and smoke drifted toward the ceiling. As I backed up, I discovered the exit, a thin space in the wall that slid open at my touch.

Cries echoed as I pulled it shut behind me, smearing stardust across the door, hoping to keep them trapped.

It was only as I fled down the hall that I realized I'd forgotten my mask. I was certain Alder was still alive, and I only had moments until he sent his elites to hunt me down. I was no match for them without stardust, but I needed a mask so I could blend in, and, most importantly, I needed to find Asira.

Sneaking through the kitchens, I flinched a mask one of the servants had left behind. It did not match my robes, but I had little time to concern myself with fashion.

I burst into the hall, moving down the tables, trying to appear casual as I moved into the dance floor, weaving between the couples, searching.

Where was she? Jabel had said she'd be in Iscariot's room, but that was before they'd discovered my identity. Alder would go there first. My chest seized, and I bolted out of the hall, drunken laughter following me.

The passageway back to the chamber seemed endless. With my heart in my throat, I burst into the room. It was empty, no signs of a struggle, just the way I'd left it. I dashed into the washroom and scoured the three rooms. Had I beaten them there?

If they'd stolen Asira away, I had to find her. My chest burned at the idea of her being in their hands, and a bolt of fury clouded my vision. I was acting out of fear and not planning carefully. If I were to win, I needed to take a deep breath and make a plan.

Fingers trembling, I went to the wardrobe and packed a bag with necessities. Once I found Asira, I would spirit her away, back to Terrin or somewhere else where she'd be safe from all this hellishness.

Knife in hand, I made my way back to the tunnels. It was no use hiding anymore or pretending to be Iscariot. Bitter thoughts swirled of poisoning their food and drink with stardust, for demons did not deserve to live. While I searched for Asira, I would damn them all.

# 21
## ASIRA

I must have nodded off, for I woke with a start, neck stiff, as though I'd fallen asleep at my table again. Blinking to clear my hazy vision, I took in the pale sunlight and the empty hut, the door still ajar, just as I'd left it.

By some stroke of luck, whoever dwelled here had not returned, likely too carried away at the celebration the eve before. I had to be gone by the time they returned and watch out for the flying beast.

My body ached when I stood, and I hesitantly applied more stardust as I snuck out of the home. Fully dressed, with a blanket around my shoulders, I found it almost pleasant outside.

A lush green lawn stretched as far as my eyes could see, and blue waterfalls sparkled in the distance. Sunshine yellow butterflies flitted around pink and white flowers, the trees thick with foliage that hadn't fallen yet.

I made a fist. The floating islands were a paradise, ruined by those foul demons. A surge of determination rose within, and I marched toward the strip of land. I was going to steal one of their chariots and fly away.

Back on the main island, I snuck toward the palace, grateful for the tree coverage. Aside from the faint thunder of falling water and the occasional wind rustling through the tree branches, nothing else reminded me of home.

At my cottage, I was used to the sound of birdsong, the chattering of the woodland creatures, the sound of footsteps hastening to my cottage to beg me to help. Here, there was no birdsong or woodland creatures, only thunder and that terrible, eerie silence.

A nasty smell rose to meet me as I got closer. It wasn't as strong as it had been inside the palace, but it still lingered, a smell I called death and rot. My stomach knotted again at the reminder of the demons, but moments later, I burst out of the forest onto a knoll.

Immediately, I stepped back, for the knoll led to a cliff, and in front of me were three Masters with chariots and horses, unloading items and tossing them over the cliff. Peering out from behind the tree, I squinted against the light, making out the items.

My skin prickled.

Bones.

White bones with no flesh, the kind I tried not to look at when I was in the boneyard collecting stardust.

The Masters pulled a body from the chariot that wasn't all bone, and my heart plummeted. I gripped the tree branch so hard, the bark made indentions on my palm and my breath turned shallow.

I knew that person.

Charlotte.

She'd been chosen only last year, but a few years earlier, she'd fallen ill with body sores and a terrible cough. Her mother and father thought she might die. I'd sat with her through the night while she lingered on the edge of life and death. Eventually, she responded to the tincture and began to heal. She'd recovered fully, and now…

Now, the Masters had killed her.

She was young, vibrant, given a second chance at life only for it to be snatched away. She was only a few years younger than me, and tears of anger burned my eyes.

I snatched the vial of stardust from around my throat, holding up the bottle, ready to throw it.

This was what the Masters did.

They came to kill and steal and destroy. They weren't our saviors protecting us from the monsters, but our jailers, and someone had to stop them.

That someone would be me, except I needed more stardust.

I imagined myself stealing one of the chariots and riding it down to my cottage, where I'd collect the remaining buckets of stardust. I'd return and rain them down on the Masters, burning each and every one of them.

Darkness surged in my chest, and my fists tightened around the vial as I took a step forward.

A whisper filled the air. “Asira.”

It came from behind me, and I felt a zing, an intense sensation of relief and joy as I spun around.

Eyes shining, Drazhan walked toward me.

# 22

# DRAZHAN

Asira. I hadn't been able to find her anywhere. I'd spent a sleepless night roaming the palace, entering rooms, leaving stardust where I'd gone until my hands were empty and there was only one place I dared not look: the place where they dumped the bodies.

Surely not.

They had a reason for capturing her. Would they kill her so quickly just to hurt me? Had she died due to their violence?

It happened sometimes, although Alder was displeased and punished those who cared so little for human life. Dead humans served no purpose, and Alder was adamant that they should be kept alive at all costs.

As I crept to the cliffside, she appeared, back to me, dressed in one of my own robes, the sun shining like gold on her head. My throat swelled up tight, making it difficult to whisper her name. She must have heard me, for she turned, pressed a finger to her lips, and pointed.

Just beyond her, the Masters were tossing bones over the cliff.

Blurred memories returned, of being stabbed by Iscariot, the life draining away from me as I was tied up, then dragged to the edge. I didn't recall being tossed over, but that's how I'd ended up in the boneyard.

Why did she have to discover this ugly secret?

Staying quiet, I crept to her side. Up close, tears streaked her cheeks, and when I slid my arms around her, she did not resist.

"Asira," I murmured again. "I thought they'd taken you and..." I trailed off, unable to say the terrible words.

A hiss came from her throat, and she pushed me away.

Behind us came the sound of wings, and the chariots lifted up, taking the Masters with them.

I watched, ensuring they did not spy us under the tree coverage, but they quickly disappeared, leaving us alone in that haunted place.

"I left," Asira said.

Even though she'd pushed me away, she kept one hand on my arm, holding tight to the sleeve of my robe. She didn't want me to hold her, but she wanted me close. I'd take what I could get.

She bit her lower lip but wouldn't hold my gaze. "You were right. The Masters are demons. I saw for myself, and I ran."

"You've been out here all night?"

Asira shook her head. "No, a flying beast caught me and dropped me on one of the adjoining islands. I found a home in the hillside and hid there until morning. I came back to steal a chariot and return to Terrin, but then I saw..." she pointed to the cliff. "They are killers. They are evil."

"I know." I cupped her cheek with my hand, surprised when she closed her eyes and leaned into me. "I spent all night searching. I'd thought the worse, but you're here. I'll take you back to Terrin—"

"No." Asira jerked away. "I'm not leaving. There's a reason the Masters choose me, and I will make it their biggest mistake. I'm staying, and this time, I'm going to help you destroy them with stardust."

My first thought was a hard and furious *no*, but wasn't this what I had wanted all along? Help to defeat this formidable foe?

I'd laid the groundwork, but I couldn't do everything by myself. I needed help, especially from one with fae blood. Asira was a healer, and I didn't want her caught in this mess, this trap. I knew what they did to those they caught, and the idea of her being in their hands was more than I could bear. I'd just gotten her back, but the truth lay before me.

I'd done nothing to assist her. She'd escaped the palace by herself and endured a night in the cold, proving she was resourceful and could take care of herself. Hadn't she, in fact, saved me?

I sighed. "Everything within me wants to say no, but I also know you are stubborn and likely to do what you want, regardless of what I say or think. It's not safe here; we should go where we can talk. The Masters know I'm not Iscariot, and soon, they'll discover you are missing. They'll search for you today."

"Where should we hide? We also need more stardust."

"It seems you've already found my hiding place."

Asira raised her eyebrows. "The home in the hillside is yours?"

I nodded.

Her shoulders sagged. "What about that beast?"

"The flying bird? That was likely Egon or one of the other dragon birds. They dwell in the mountain ranges up here."

Asira made a face. "Your pet?"

"No, he's more wild than tame."

"Well, his talons are sharp. He ripped up my side."

"You're wounded?" No wonder she pushed me away so quickly.

She nodded. "Nothing a little stardust won't heal."

"I'm afraid all the stardust we have left is in your vial."

"Nonsense. I have more at my cottage. In fact, my plan was to steal a chariot, take the rest of it, and return here to punish the Masters."

Blood roared in my ears. What had my impatience and fear wrought? I pinched my nose between my fingers. "I took all of it during my search for you last night, and I lined the palace with stardust."

Asira's eyes narrowed. "What do you mean? What happens now?"

"Ideally, the stardust will cause the air in the palace to become toxic, and the Masters will sicken and die. It's only a matter of time."

"Are you sure it was all of it?"

"No, but I was angry. I thought they had you."

Asira let go of me, her expression softening, eyes lost as she stared at the ground. "I don't understand. I'm just the Stardust Collector."

"To me, you're so much more."

# 23
## ASIRA

Back in the home in the hillside, Drazhan unloaded his bag, taking out a warm gown for me, along with a fur-lined cloak. "These were in Iscariot's chambers and will keep you warm against the chill. I'll be just outside, finding wood for a fire."

I took the clothes, surprised at this thoughtfulness. "Won't lighting a fire be dangerous? What if the Masters aren't dying from stardust, and they come to find us?"

"It is a risk, but we need to eat to keep up our strength. Besides, there are hidden routes we can use to disappear. Dress and use more of the stardust on your wound. I'll return shortly."

Drazhan slipped out the door, and it was not lost on me how our roles were reversed. Now, I was the one wounded, healing in his home while he worked and made food for me. How quickly things changed. I was so relieved to see him again, albeit slightly disappointed that he hadn't tried to kiss me yet.

When he'd embraced me, part of me longed to stay in his arms, but the friction against my broken skin hurt. I'd pushed him away, but part of me also didn't want to admit that I felt something else, a budding heat, a flicker of flame, that same weightless sensation I felt whenever he kissed me.

When the door opened, I stared at him with fresh eyes, all judgment cast aside.

Drazhan wasn't one of the Masters. He was someone else, a protector from another realm, tall and handsome with a flirtatious wink in his golden eyes.

He'd told me a tale of a place that defied knowledge, as though he were used to living in cities in the sky. Once, he'd brought down an entire city, and he aimed to do it again. When he was done here, what would happen next?

"You're staring at me," Drazhan said. "Should I be concerned?"

I watched the power in his arms as he swung a load off his back, set a pot on the fire, and started chopping vegetables for soup.

"No, I was just thinking."

"Thinking of?"

I settled on the pallet and leaned against the earthy wall, watching Drazhan light the fire with just a few words. Magic.

"I don't want to go back," I said softly, the confession hanging like a dagger between us.

Those golden eyes held mine just a moment before he returned to his work. "Back where? And why?"

"Back home, to my cottage in the woods. I don't want to be the Stardust Collector anymore. In truth, when I asked you to ensure I was chosen, it wasn't because I wished to be up here. I did, of course, but I wanted a change, something different. For as long as I can remember, my family line has dwelled in Terrin with the unique task of being the healers of the land, the Stardust Collectors. It's a long and lonely task and...

boring. Every year, I do the same thing, help the same people, collect the stardust and herbs, make tinctures, and go to town, but mostly, I wait for something, anything, to happen in my humble life. The only change I could conceive of was being chosen, invited to dwell here, and now that I'm here, now that I've learned the truth, I feel...powerful."

Drazhan stilled, his expression unreadable. "Powerful. That's not the word I expected to hear from your lips. Maybe frightened or angry, but not...powerful."

I rubbed the soft material of the cloak, unable to look at him. "It sounds terrible. As a healer, I help the people of Terrin, and I'm aware that their lives are a little less burdensome because of the knowledge I carry. It's all written down, though. It doesn't *have* to be me. Being up here is terrifying, and I do feel anger and fear, but mainly, I feel rage. The Masters pretended to protect Terrin. I can help stop the madness, and that knowledge makes me feel more alive than I have in years."

"There is no greater power than life and death, and as a healer, you hold that power. Still, you want more, to liberate those from evil."

"Yes."

"But the people of Terrin don't know who the Masters truly are."

I shook my head. "No, but there is an aura of fear in Terrin, of doubt and mistrust. Something is wrong. Everyone feels it, and everyone looks to the skies with hope. Everyone wants to be chosen because it means escape and a better life. What if the fall of the Masters is enough for them to realize that we can have a better life without living up here? What if the floating islands were open to all, to come and go as they please?"

"You dream of the future. I knew I liked you."

Drazhan slid the vegetables into the pot and joined me on the pallet. He tapped my head gently. "You're like no one I've ever met. You're not content to sit in one place your entire life. I made a promise to you, and I will keep it. If it's an adventure you want, the chance to impact the world on a much larger scale, then you shall have it."

My lips trembled, but I forced myself to meet his gaze and see the sincerity there. "It seems anticlimactic to sit here and wait while the Masters do who knows what."

"True. After we eat and rest, we shall see what has become of them. Right now, though, I'd very much like to kiss you."

I sucked in a deep breath, aware of his proximity and how much I wanted another one of his earth-shattering kisses. When his lips were pressed against mine, it was as if the entire world faded away. "Why do you like to kiss me so much?"

Drazhan took a loose curl and twirled it around his fingertip. "Because when I kiss you, it feels like we are lost souls meant to find each other. When I kiss you, it feels like home, that everything is all right, exactly as it was meant to be."

Moisture gathered behind my eyes, and I tugged him closer, this time taking the opportunity to initiate the kiss. Closing my eyes, I let myself go and pressed my lips against his, welcoming him, tasting him.

I let my fingers explore, resting against his powerful jawline, feeling the rough stubble of his beard. One hand drifted lower, resting against his thudding heartbeat.

A bloom of emotion rose inside my chest. I was wanted, not for what I could do for others or my skills, but simply for being myself.

My breath hitched as I pulled back, meeting his smoldering gaze. "It's time, Drazhan. I'd like to share my bed with you."

# 24
## DRAZHAN

Asira's touch sent shudders of joy through my soul as we made love. I closed my eyes, enjoying every moment, the way her fingers trailed down my body, her moans of pleasure, the needy, urgent way she kissed me.

Together, we explored the heights of pleasure, and when it was over, I held her close. Her eyes slipped shut, long lashes sweeping her cheeks, and a look of utter bliss across those lips. Ever so gently, I tucked her head against my shoulder and held her.

"Rest," I whispered. "Rest."

She didn't respond, and I wondered if I'd sent her to the land of dreams. A sudden exhaustion came over me. I hadn't slept last night, but here, safe with my beloved, I felt at peace.

The scent of vegetable soup filled the air, along with a faint breeze and the distant thunder of waterfalls. I closed my eyes and let go at last.

When I woke, the fire had gone out, and Asira knelt over the pot, spooning soup into two bowls. When I sat up, she smiled at me, which only made her appear more relaxed and beautiful. She held up a bowl.

"Hungry? We slept most of the day."

"Good." I accepted the bowl from her and lifted it to my lips, blowing gently on the hot liquid. "Under the cover of nightfall is the ideal time to return to the palace to see if any are left alive."

Asira shuddered.

"You don't have to come," I started, then trailed off at her glare. Of course, she was coming.

"Actually, I have a question for you."

"Ask," I encouraged.

Asira cupped the bowl in her hands and took a drink before speaking. "I'm curious why the Masters chose me this time. From what I heard, they specifically wanted the Stardust Collector. Surely, the Masters are aware that stardust is harmful to them, yet it falls once a year. I've always wondered: where does the stardust come from?"

A cold sensation went through me at her words, and suddenly, I knew the truth. Asira wasn't chosen because they wanted her to extend the line of Masters. No, it was for another reason that only now made sense to me. "Asira, I have much to tell you."

"The night is young," she quipped.

"Every year, on All Hallow's Eve, there is a cleansing ceremony in preparation for the tithe. The Masters get rid of all the old bones they've kept throughout the year, and when they do so, a strange phenomenon happens: stardust falls. No one can explain it. Some call it the tears from the sky, weeping over the dead."

Asira shivered. "Creepy. What about the legend of monsters?

I finished my soup and set the bowl aside. "Perhaps there once were monsters beyond the mountains, and perhaps they are still there now, but they have shown no interest in coming here or attacking this land. Yesterday, when I was in the inner sanctum, they spoke of the war with the fae, their diminished numbers, and how they were clever enough to harness the power of flight and flee from the known world."

"So, each year stardust falls, but no one can explain why. There might not be monsters, and the Masters are telling a lie so the people of Terrin will worship them?"

"I think the so-called monsters the Masters are saving us from are, in actuality, the fae."

Asira pressed her lips together. "Did you know about their demonic appearance?"

I shook my head. "I did not. If I had to guess, the drug they gave you is to help them retain their glamour, making them appear like myself, or angels. The stardust displays their true form, and when they touch it, it burns them."

"Yes, I discovered that yesterday. Going back to my earlier question – why me?"

"The Masters are well aware that stardust is used in Terrin, that it has magical healing properties. I believe they called you here because you know the secrets of stardust and you are a healer."

She looked at me. "But why? Who needs to be healed here?"

"In the coming months, two children will be born. I believe the Masters wanted you to be present for the births, to ensure the babies are born healthy."

Asira's eyes went wide, and she sat down her bowl. "Oh." She wrinkled her nose. "We have to find the mothers and save them, whoever they are."

"We will."

"Drazhan, I'm concerned about Terrin. From what you've told me, when the Masters are gone, the stardust will disappear, and there will no longer be a need for a Stardust Collector."

Asira saw truth so quickly. I moved to her side and squeezed her hand. "Correct."

"If there's no stardust, the magic that heals the people will be gone."

"Yes, Terrin will become like other lands that don't have magic, but you said it yourself: there won't be a need for stardust. You have a book of herbs and mixtures that will help others to heal."

"True, but a pinch of stardust does far more than anything else." She touched her side. "In less than a day, my wound has closed. Even though I still feel pain, it is healing much faster than it would without stardust."

"Then you must make a choice for Terrin. What is worse? Living under the thumb of the Masters and their hideous secrets, or a life without stardust?"

She sighed. "The Masters are the greater evil."

"Then you have your answer."

Asira faced me. "I do, although the weight of that knowledge sits heavy on my shoulders."

"That is the flip side of power: it comes with that weight of responsibility. I will gladly bear that weight with you."

“It’s still heavy, even when shared,” Asira said, and then, in the most surprising move, she leaned over and kissed me.

# 25
## ASIRA

Silver moonlight shone in as Drazhan pressed a knife into my hands. "Just in case. We don't know what we're walking into. If all goes well, we enter a tomb and need to do nothing more than set the prisoners free."

I squeezed the blade and nodded. I'd used a knife plenty of times.

I followed Drazhan outside, glancing at the skies in case the dragon bird, Egon, was awake and choose to pounce on us. I'd seen giant birds, but from the distance, I'd assumed they were eagles or hawks, just unnaturally large. I hadn't believed in dragons until now.

Recalling Drazhan's story about the Sky Watch, I wondered if Egon was the kind of dragon that breathed fire, although it was unlikely any would dwell on an island where dragon fire might doom them all.

I expected to creep across the strip of land connecting the islands, but Drazhan had other ideas. He moved further into the island to a statue. At the base, he slid open a secret door, revealing a step of steps into the ground.

"These stairs lead to the tunnels," he explained. "I use them to sneak around the islands unseen. The network of tunnels also leads to the palace, and while the Masters use them, they dislike the cold and dark. It reminds them of where they came from."

I stared at the darkness, my fury rising again.

The trap door shut behind us and Drazhan handed me a round ball of light. "We have to stay quiet, just in case," he warned.

I nodded, blade in one hand, heart in my throat. I would have felt better if I had stardust, knowing what it could do.

The path in the dark seemed to trail on endlessly. We came to a few crossroads, but Drazhan always knew which way to go.

At last, the air shifted, the scent going from earthy to that stench of rot and death. My insides curled at the memory of red eyes and molted skin. What horrors were we about to stumble upon?

Drazhan motioned for me to wait as he climbed a ladder. A faint glow came as he lifted a trap door then waved for me to join him. He disappeared above, and I hesitated before reminding myself that the Masters were monsters, and I had joined Drazhan's cause to bring them to justice.

Up the ladder, I found myself in a large kitchen, quiet and empty. Abandoned. Because it was night or for some other reason?

Goblets were strewn about, and an overturned bottle of wine dripped into the floor, the puddle like a stain of blood. I lifted my chin. It was time to free the chosen ones.

We moved down the silent halls, our steps loud in the quiet, but I couldn't shake the sense that we were being watched. No bodies lay on the floor as I expected, and the torches that lit up the halls were still lit. Had they taken the dead and fled?

Then came a sound, like a stick striking the ground. We were at the great hall, which had once been so vibrant with life and full of song. I peeked in the doorway, almost surprised to see the darkness of the room.

A cold voice came, weaving through the velvet blackness. "So, you thought to cause us harm, to destroy us with stardust. Come. See what you have wrought."

Lights came from everywhere at once. I sucked in a deep breath, wanting to flee, but my feet were stuck to the ground, staring in horror.

Blood covered the walls, ruining the murals and tapestries. Even the chandeliers, glinting with crystals, were stained red, giving an amber glow to the lights. A demon stood on the stage, withered and bent with age, and around him was a sea of unmasked demons.

Despite the light, their bulbous eyes glowed. Fangs glinted in the light, and those who had tails swished them, eager for a fight. I gulped, bravery gone as I stared at their mishappen appearances. Some were missing fingers or toes, and there were others with chunks of their bodies missing, even faces half-rotted away.

The effects of stardust. Drazhan had greatly damaged the Masters, but he hadn't been able to kill them all. The remnants stood tall, waiting to finish us off.

They weren't the only ones in the room, for golden cages full of the Chosen lined the walls. They must have been drugged, for they stared out of empty eyes or lay sleeping.

"You've come to free the humans, haven't you, Drazhan? You didn't count on us finding a cure for stardust."

A cure? No. Not possible. The one weapon that was supposed to save us was rendered useless. Otherwise, how else would the demons be standing before us? My little knife was laughable.

"Run," Drazhan's command came in my ear. "I'll distract them. Get back to the tunnels, as far away as possible. Run."

My numb feet sprang to life. Spinning on my heels, I dashed back the way we'd come. Behind me came a roar.

"Seize them!"

I raked my mind for answers as my feet pounded the floor. The still-healing wound in my side ached from the quick movement. I glanced behind me, heart pounding as the demons poured out of the hall and surged after us like a storm.

The fae. How did the fae beat the Masters? I had fae blood, but it was useless without the secret. The words on the scroll came dancing back: *...they laid their hands upon the Masters and damned them.*

I must have made a wrong turn because I couldn't find the kitchen, or the trap door. Suddenly, Drazhan was at my side. "This way," he said, and we burst out of the palace.

Once again, I found myself fleeing down the garden path while they chased after me, but this time, there was no hope, no remedy. They'd discovered how to protect themselves against stardust, which meant we'd failed.

If they caught us, they'd kill us.

Cold air slapped my face, but I only imagined the putrid breath of those demons, claws flaying skin from bone and curved teeth devouring all.

Something warm dripped down my side. Blood. My wound had re-opened. Pain spread from my side up my spine, and my breath turned labored, my steps slow and dragging.

I pressed my hands against my side until they were slick with blood, and the realization dawned on me that this was the end. I wouldn't escape, and Drazhan should have a second chance. This was his moment, his vengeance, yet somehow, we'd both failed.

My feet slowed to a stop and my shoulders sagged. Dimly, I heard Drazhan shouting. "Asira, come on. Just a few more feet. You can do this!"

My vision swirled and then cleared as the volley of shouts roared in my ears. I lifted my bloody hands from my side and a stillness came over me, a surge of determination.

I could not say where it had come from. I wasn't a warrior, and I had no magic. I was simply a mortal, a Stardust Collector with a skill for healing, and fae blood running through my veins.

An overwhelming peace came over me, as though I was exactly where I needed to be, and fear could not reach me. A victorious shout came as the demons surrounded me and a wave of something beyond me, a power not quite my own, filled my body.

I lifted my bloody hands as the demons reached me, howling as they surged around me, ready to rip me to shreds. I smelled their anger, their desperation for revenge, and worst of all, their evilness.

They came for blood, they came to kill, steal, and destroy. Worst of all, they enjoyed it.

# 26
## DRAZHAN

A cure for stardust. The words rang in my mind as we fled, although Asira quickly fell behind. We were almost to another entrance to the tunnels when she stopped and faced them. Even I knew how difficult they were to kill, and the knife I'd given her would only slow them down, not stop them.

I spun around, drawing my sword as they surrounded her. "Asira!" I screamed, my heart squeezing.

The crowd of demons roared with glee as they surrounded her, counting on an easy kill. Closing my eyes, I summoned my magic. A burst of speed and power came over me as I dived into the fray. Tearing and ripping, I stabbed my way toward her.

"Asira!"

They would not take her too.

Demons went flying, and then a boom of thunder smote the air. Something heavy fell on my shoulders, and I went down, squirming as I tried to free myself.

Another boom came, followed by howls of pain and fear. The demons were frightened.

As I crawled out from under the heavy object, silence met my ears. Gingerly, I stood, and my knife slipped from my fingers as I stared.

All around me were stone statues of demons.

My jaw dropped.

The demons had turned to stone, and in the distance, those who escaped were running, not toward the palace, but away, deeper into the floating islands.

I touched one of the statues, still warm but heavy, solid stone.

“Asira?” I called, straining to find her in the garden of stone demons.

“I’m here,” came her voice, tinged with awe.

I spun around, and there she was, her side wet with blood but a light shining in her eyes. One lip curled back, she lifted her hands. “The secret of the fae was the blood. All they had to do was lay their hands on the Masters, and they turned them to stone.”

The words from the scroll drifted back to my mind. The answer had been in front of us the entire time, and Asira had finally unlocked it, saving Terrin and the chosen ones.

She wavered, and I dashed to her side, holding her as she slumped against me. “You did it,” I whispered.

Her lips curved up in a half smile. “*We* did it.”

# 27
## ASIRA

The next three days passed in a blur. Drazhan and I worked together to free the chosen ones, help restore them to full health, and then send them back to the ground on golden chariots. I convinced Drazhan he should be the one to announce the change to the people of Terrin.

Once again, the people gathered, just like they did on the day of the tithe, and Drazhan announced that the Masters had fled, leaving Terrin in the hands of the people. He even went so far as to dismantle the knights and tell the people to build a democracy.

They were stunned, and I imagined it would be a while before they figured out what to do. Part of me felt I needed to stay to help guide the people of

Terrin through the change. The other part of me was anxious, fearing I'd be forced to return to my job as a healer now that my adventure was over.

I hadn't had an opportunity to catch Drazhan alone, but now, I wandered through the palaces gardens to where Drazhan stood near the edge of the floating island, watching the last of the winged horses fly away.

Standing by his side, I watched the horses speed away into cloud and mist. "Do you think they'll return?" I asked.

"Perhaps," Drazhan said, taking my hand. "The islands are empty now, and I expect more wildlife will make this place their home."

"I have a question for you, Drazhan."

He faced me, an eyebrow raised.

"About your magic."

"You assume I have magic."

"Don't all Masters have magic? Or is that another falsehood, like iron?"

He sighed. "Truthfully, I do have magic, but not the kind you're thinking of. Mine is for simple, everyday use, like lighting a fire or making water boil. I am stronger than mortals, and at times, magic gives me incredible speed. That is all."

I pressed my lips together, glancing at the cascade of colors in the sky. "When the Masters turned to stone, I felt a surge of power, and I thought it might have come from you."

Drazhan's golden eyes turned serious. "I have a theory, Asira, about your power, your magic. You have fae blood, which makes you unique, and you've worked with stardust daily. Stardust has magical properties, and you've absorbed so much of it, the magic is within you. While stardust slowed down the demons, your touch was more powerful. That's why you woke me in the boneyard, and why I healed so quickly. We both believed it was stardust, but all along, it was you. You're the magic of Terrin, and as long as you dwell here, stardust will never truly be gone."

A lump swelled in my throat. Drazhan had so much faith in me. I squeezed his hand. "I believe you're right. It's quite a revelation. I wanted to come here to discover the truth, and I did. Still though, some of the Masters escaped."

"I've been thinking about that too. I must go hunt them down. It is my task, after all, to hunt down evil, vanquish demons, and bring freedom to the oppressed."

I hesitated. "When do you leave?"

"The sooner the better." Drazhan drew me into his arms, cupping my face with his warm hands. "But I'm not ready to leave you behind just yet. As I recall, I promised when I finished my task up that I'd return for you."

I smiled at him. "I do worry about you going off alone, fighting to defeat evil without a healer by your side."

"You? Worry? Thought I'd never hear those words from you."

I giggled. "I did find you half dead in a boneyard."

"This is true. There's only one way to keep me safe. I need a healer by my side at all times. Would you like to come with me? I think you're rather adept at the task."

I smirked. "Will there be more demons?"

"Probably."

"I'm assuming there will be lots of danger and darkness."

Drazhan shrugged. "I can't help that."

"Doesn't sound safe for a woman like me," I teased.

"No, I can't promise you safety. Only adventure, magic, kisses, and my heart."

I blinked, my words faltering. "Your heart?"

Drazhan lowered his voice. "Yes. After all, love is a powerful magic. Now, are you coming or..."

I laced my fingers around his neck and rose up on my tiptoes. "My answer was yes all along. I was just testing you."

"I knew that."

I smiled. "Did you? You started to get teary-eyed."

"Actually, you're the one who got teary-eyed when I told you how I feel about you."

"Well," I countered, "I've lived alone for a long time. It's not every day I find a stranger who changes my perspective."

"So, you feel the same way?"

"I thought it was obvious."

When his lips brushed mine, my chest tingled, like wings fluttering against my ribcage.

Stardust would no longer fall in Terrin, but the people were free, and I'd discovered my power, a purpose, and best of all, Drazhan.

# WHAT TO READ NEXT

Enjoyed this story but want more? Check out the Tower Knights collection: complete, stand-alone spicy fantasy romances.

Phantom of the Opera meets Beauty and the Beast in this gothic-inspired dark fantasy romance.

*A haunted tower, a mysterious instructor, and the lure of the music of the night...*

**Get a discount on signed hardcovers when you visit angelajford.com**

# Also by Angela J. Ford

Join my email list for updates, previews, giveaways, and new release notifications. Join now: www.angelajford.com/signup

**Chronicles of the Four Worlds (epic fantasy)**

*A complete six-book epic fantasy series spanning two hundred years, featuring an epic battle between mortals and immortals.*

**Legend of the Nameless One Series (epic fantasy)**

*A complete five-book epic fantasy adventure series featuring an enchantress, a wizard, and a sarcastic dragon.*

**Night of the Dark Fae Trilogy (romantic epic fantasy)**

*A complete epic fantasy trilogy featuring a strong heroine, dark fae, orcs, goblins, dragons, antiheroes, magic, and romance.*

**Tales of the Enchanted Wildwood (fairy tale romance)**

*Adult fairy tales blending fantasy action-adventure with steamy romance. Each short story can be read as a stand-alone and features a different couple.*

**Tower Knights (fantasy romance)**

*Gothic-inspired adult steamy fantasy romance. Each novel can be read as a stand-alone and features a different couple.*

**Gods & Goddesses of Labraid (epic fantasy)**

*A complete epic fantasy duology featuring a warrior princess with a dire future who embarks on a perilous quest to regain her fallen kingdom.*

**Lore of Nomadia Trilogy (epic fantasy romance)**

*The story of an alluring nymph, a curious librarian, a renowned hunter, and a mad sorceress as they seek to save—or destroy—the empire of Nomadia.*

**One Winter Night (fantasy romance)**

*Winter-themed spicy fantasy romance. Each novel is a stand-alone and features a difference couple.*

Visit angelajford.com for autographed books, exclusive book swag and book boxes.

# ABOUT THE AUTHOR

Angela J. Ford is a bestselling author who writes epic fantasy and steamy fantasy romance with vivid worlds, gray characters and endings you just can't guess.

Aside from writing she and her husband own The Signed Book Shop. A one-stop shop for readers to find signed books and book merchandise.

If you happen to be in Nashville, you'll most likely find her enjoying a white chocolate mocha and daydreaming about her next book.


facebook.com/angelajfordauthor

instagram.com/angelajfordbooks

amazon.com/Angela-J-Ford/e/B0052U9PZO

bookbub.com/authors/angela-j-ford